I HAD ALSO LOVED SOMEONE

Nitish Raj

Become
Shakespeare
.com

First published in 2018 by

Becomeshakespeare.com
Wordit Content Design & Editing Services Pvt Ltd
Unit - 26, Building A-1, Nr Wadala RTO, Wadala (East),
Mumbai 400037, India
T:+91 8080226699
This book has been funded by WORDIT ART FUND
WORDIT ART FUND helps deserving
Authors publish their work
To apply for funding, please visit us at
becomeshakespeare.com

©
ISBN: 978-93-86487-85-8

Disclaimer
This is a work of fiction. Names, characters, business,
place, event and incidents are either the product of the
author's imagination or used in a fictitious manner. Any
resemblance to actual person, living or dead or actual
event is purely coincidental.

PREFACE

The most sought-after three magical words "I Love You" which we have all been aware of at any point of time of our life seems losing its' charm and magic. Love which used to be a pious virtue seems to be transforming into lust which is not only liable for shattering our hearts but also giving birth to such immoral acts which perhaps would not be even forgiven in the courts of the Almighty. Perhaps the Almighty either willingly or unwillingly defies the sobs of the wretched heart otherwise how could it happen that for the person whom we are ready to lay our life is not even worthy of our hatred.

Even though today we claim to be modern, globalized and a hell lot of other things, we have not been able to pay the deserved respect to the better half of the society. Had it been the case, we would have remain unheard of one of the most barbarous act; gang rape which could be never done by someone who loves to call himself human? It could be lasciviousness, prurient act or diseased mentality but certainly not a human trait. Not only those vicious scoundrels but our society is also equally responsible in humiliating the victims to the maximum extent.

I have just tried to make an attempt to restore the piousness of the sacred love which seems to be losing somewhere with every passing day. The gang rape victims who are the prey of some peccant perverts need not to be either on the mercy of the society or those crooks who consider such acts as an achievement. The victims do not have the necessity to verify themselves from this society as they are the victorious warriors who have a lot to say instead of being a prey of the satires of this rotten society.

FOREWORD

If there is something in particular which I look forward to when I enter a book store, it is a book from a new voice. There's almost always a certain magical rawness about an author's debut work. There's nothing like discovering a fresh voice whose storytelling prowess pulls you like none other. I feel privileged to write a foreword to one such voice, Nitish Raj, who I'm sure in coming times will not only leave a deep imprint in the publishing industry but also in the hearts of those who savor his work.

When Nitish told me about the book and the core issue he is handling through the story, I was immediately interested. Being a thriller author myself the prospect of a woman serial killer was supremely alluring. Later when I found out the book deals with rape and its individual trauma alongside the societal reflex towards the victim I was insanely hooked. I think the timing of the release of this book couldn't have been better. A topical crime thriller is always a winner since people use their social experience to relate to the protagonist's emotional graph. It's all the more necessary to present stories which are a reflection of the current social on goings since it generates more empathy in people towards the social issue or the victim of it. I'm happy Nitish understood this before venturing out as a storyteller.

Any debut author would have chosen a safer story to begin since building one's own readership is as important as telling a new story for an author. But I'm glad Nitish with this debut work of his showed not only his intention of keeping some 'take away' for those readers who want to read a story for its gravity but also told it in a thriller genre to keep the entertainment quotient high. The best balance of such elements actually give rise to great books.

By choosing a woman protagonist in his debut work Nitish did take up a challenge since when a man writes from a woman's point of view, that too someone who has been at a receiving end of a dastardly attack it's an uphill task. Rape is such a heinous invasion of a person's privacy that we, more of often than not, can only sympathize but never empathize. To write about such a sensitive issue and jacketing it within the garb of a thriller to drive home a social issue is something which Nitish had done with utmost finesse considering this is his first novel.

I would take this opportunity to wish Nitish all the very best for the road ahead which I'm sure would be as exciting as it would be challenging. And he would churn out more stories which not only reflect the naked truth of the society but also engages us all as we read on.

Novoneel Chakraborty
Bestselling Author

ACKNOWLEDGEMENT

Before even writing a single syllable I would like to be thankful to the Almighty who showered His immense blessings on me which left me surrounded with such great people till now. May god bless every child with such parents who sacrifice their own life for their child. Whether it be my father or my mother (Whom I lovingly call "Maate") who took great pains in shaping my ideologies and thought-process. I would be indebted for my whole life to Prof. Akram Hoque who not only believed in my words but also acted as a mentor. I would also love to thanks my editor, Umesh Prasad Chaudhary who through his valuable feedback polished the manuscript.

Last but not the least, I would love to thanks the whole team of BecomeShakespeare.com especially to Likhita Puthran; Project Manager and Pooja Dutt; Publishing Associate who put their immense hardwork in making my brainchild a reality.

PART-1

Prologue

❊ ❊ ❊

Present Day (11th March; 07:30 A.M)

"Hey! Niharika; will you say something or continue staring me like a witch?"

"Nope!" Her words were filled with a sang-froid attitude.

"Think properly, otherwise you would not get any chance again. It's my kind-heartedness that I am asking otherwise no other officials would have asked you. No one is allowed to even have a talk with you as in just a matter of three hours you will go for final hearing and even if you try hard you can't escape this time."

"Hmm…"

"Are you insane or what that I am talking to you and you are just giving me a one word answer? I understand that you are fearful of the punishment which you are sure to get. But you should have thought this before that why I am doing such a nasty thing? Really! You would always remain a case study for me that a girl who is a nulli secun dus beauty can also be so much dangerous and even so much stubborn that she has not even the basic etiquette that one should reply in a proper manner when an elder person is trying to talk to you…"

"Hmm…"

"Oh! Nothing could happen with this girl. I am wasting my time on this girl. I should better go."

And the police officer went from her little cell abusing her in his sub-conscious mind.

Was I really such a girl who is so much nasty that had not a slight degree of etiquette? Was I such a girl who is insane and a girl who is just pretty by face with ulterior motives in her mind? No! Niharika! No, Niharika Ahuja! You were also like all the common girl who had a normal life where normal and abnormal things happen on a consecutive basis. But tell me my God! When I have to be either in a top-class college or an MNC; I am sitting here in this dingy prison where I am counting my each and every seconds that when these damn three hours will pass and this damn judicial system will read some typical articles and these crook; so called lawyers will boast of their knowledge and I will be issued a death statement and nothing else. After all these craps these 'Jallads' will hang me so that I can meet my unexpected death. I have no regrets but what was the fault of this brune who is sitting beside me. She had only fulfilled the duties of a best friend but she is getting the death penalty just for helping me.

Oh! How much those days were nice when we were just best friends like other best friends who swear every day of living together and dying together? But will our those false swearing one day become real I have not even dreamt of? Niharika! You had not even dreamt of where you have reached today? People would have been thinking that I am terrified but I have neither any fear nor any regret. I was also living a life which may be dream for others before these pusillanimous creatures had transformed my life worse than a hell. All people are back-biting that I am deserved for the 'Hang Till Death' penalty but had these morons ever thought that what were the circumstances which led a girl from the balcony of the college to the grips of court-room and these all bull-shits?

"Niharika, why are you so silent?"

"No; Jasmine; I am not silent. I am thinking something."

"What; tell na!"

"Are there jasmines in heaven or not? How will I recall your name when we will get different apartments in heaven?"

"Hahaha...! You will never change."

"Yes! I will never change."

I will never change. I will never change... Never...

Chapter-1

❀ ❀ ❀

Few Years Back

"Niharika; you will never change!"

"What happened mom?"

"Your dad has spoilt you. If he wouldn't have said anything; I would have mended your ways in just a fraction of second."

"Daddy! Look, mom is again scolding me without reason."

"I am scolding you without reason. She had placed the pics of half-naked models in my novel. You do not have even a mauvaise honte on your face. Nasty girl!"

"But in your young age, you would have not been less sexy and hot than these models. Isn't it; dad?"

And before his father could speak after seizing his laughter, her mother ran towards her with a stick in her hand and she ran from there by making a clown's face and teasing her mother. It was the regular ritual of Niharika to play pranks on everyone whether it be her family, friends, classmates or teachers. As anyone couldn't determine the pattern of her jokes and pranks; it was her main strength. God knows why people feel envious of anyone's pranks but if anyone would have asked her what she get in teasing people; she always replied;

'It makes me feel bubbly and I feel happy as I do not get boredom in doing this."

And she meant her reply. If any people would have seen her from a bird's eye view she would have been seen busy only making preparation for her pranks and jokes. But as naughty and bubbly she was, she was equally intelligent and talented. She was not only the owner of a god-gifted personality but also a god-gifted mind. She was not only the topper of her class but also a very enthusiastic participant of cross-cultural activities in the school and inter-school competition. Other parents used to feel envious of her parents as they were not so lucky to get such a child who was the source of pride for their parents.

Chapter-2

❖ ❖ ❖

"Mom; I want to take admission in a B-School."

"What! Are you an idiot or what that you will take admission in a school rather than a college?"

"Oh! No. I want to take admission in a management college."

"Then what about your IIT-JEE results. You had got 438th All India Rank." His father interrupted in the middle.

"Are you insane that you will leave IIT for getting admission in the so called B-School so that you can pursue your waste passion of getting a management degree?"

"Dadddd!!........"

It was needless to say that there was almost a situation of the Second World War in her house where everyone including her own loving dad was scolding her for the first time. Her father was also right at his own place. He could not even think in his wildest dreams that her own daughter would go so much insane that she would decide to leave IIT which is a distant dream for millions of students just for the sake of getting a management degree. But this was

Niharika! She didn't care about anyone's suggestion when she gets committed to any decision and her father was very well aware of this fact. He was now just trying his hard to change the decision of her daughter so that her sweetheart could pursue a safe career instead of a highly market dependent course. This side her mother was almost hysterical when she got to know that her Niharika is refusing to get admission in one of the most premiere college of India as she does not want to spend her whole life sitting in front of a laptop decoding those programmes which no one understands except the programmer.

"But I have no money to give donation for your management."

"Dad! Do you think also like this? I have cleared the entrance also for a B-School and I am getting a 100% scholarship as I had topped that entrance examination."

Her mother's facial expression became a little bit soft after hearing that she would have not to take any loans for her study but she was not sure as she did not have much idea about this course. But her father didn't want to be blamed for not letting to pursue her dream for his whole life.

"Ok! Where is the college?"

"Pune! Symbiosis Institute Of Business Management."

"That means you will leave us and will go to Pune." Her mother cross-questioned her even without asking a question.

"Mom! Now don't start your emotional drama."

"You will never change." Her father added with half amusement and half teasing to her daughter.

"Yes! I will never change. I love you mom and dad. I love you."

Chapter-3

❋ ❋ ❋

16th August; Wednesday; 01:00 PM

Oh! How can I forget that day? This day will be imprinted in my soul even after I would become mortal. No one can erase it neither from my memory nor my heart. How much this day was beautiful for me? I had come to a new city, new world of dreams, aspirations where I will fulfil my all dreams which had remained unfulfilled in that small town of Gaya. People say that it's not a metropolitan city but is close to a metropolitan city because we have a cosmopolitan culture as the world famous Buddhist temples are located here and attract a lot of foreign tourists round the year. I don't care. This is the city which would cheer out loud on my success after three years when I would complete my BBA from here and I would be the student who would get the chance to complete her MBA from a foreign university as after that I will also clear GMAT as I had cleared this examination. Then I would select International Business as my specialisation which would give me an edge over other students and would give me an opportunity to travel the whole world. I will also learn foreign languages here which are almost impossible in this specs-claded course of so called engineers. How much beautiful it will be when I would be the first girl of my colony who will not make strange faces when any foreigner utter any language except english? People say that small town girls could not do much but they will be literally astonished when one day I would be the CEO or MD of any big MNC giant. Really, I am lucky that my parents allowed me to come so far from my home so that I can pursue my passion. I will not let them down. I will raise their head with my best performance.

"Mam, you had reached your college."

"Whattt??" She started to stumble confronting the present.

"Mam, you had reached your college."

"Oh! Thank you."

OMG! Is this my college? Really is it a college or a palace in heaven? Are the colleges are also like that? I can't believe this. Niharika! Control yourself. This is your college. You are going to spend your three years in this heaven. Am I so much lucky? Thank you God! Thank you! Thank you Niharika! Stop acting like a kid. This is the problem of girls like you who became hysterical when they reach to a big city. This is the sole reason you provide these people to make a mockery of yourself and then you blame your friends for not respecting you. No! No! I am not being hysterical. I can't believe that this type of place can be also a college. If this is the college from outside; then how would be it from inside? Ok! Now I should control my emotions and go to my hostel like a normal girl and then I would have a much better look of this paradise.

Chapter-4

❄ ❄ ❄

"Hey Jasmine, do you remember the first day in our college?"

"Yep! When you entered in the hostel, even though you were trying to remain calm; excitement was crystal clear on your face. You were pretending to be silent but your face was saying something else."

"Yar! What can I do? I was in a total exclamation after seeing the grandeur of college; I couldn't stop myself. What a college it was! Jasmine! Really I was totally surprised after entering the hostel as it was like a five-star hotel. How beautiful those beds were? It seemed that they were not less than mattresses. And you remember; I was the last girl who had come in that room? Those two witches were looking to me as if they had seen an alien. Jasmine, tell me one thing; was I really looking bad at that time? "

"My Sweety! You were looking gorgeous. You know na, metro girls always feel themselves superior without reasons."

"Hmmm…That Shweta was like a bamboo who was only tall and having no figure and that Anshu even though she was good-looking looked like a school-teacher when she used to wear spectacles. But they were really mean. They always used to protect their belongings as we were thieves and we would steal their items."

"Leave it na, what we will eat when we go to heaven? I haven't any idea of food menu of heaven."

"Hahaha…."

***

Oh! How could I leave? I had never left anything in my life. Neither those knaves, nor that seniors who tried to do ragging with us even in a B-School. I had taught that fatty a very good lesson who was trying to be over-smart as she was their so called leader only having bavardages on her lips everytime. Even I was myself in a setback to find that even though they were two years senior to me; they also felt in my trap and pranks. Niharika! You are really very mean. You shouldn't have done this. He should have at least a slight degree of knowledge that he is going to take the ragging of the 'Ragging Queen'. I had made even my teachers and my parents in a weird state with my pranks and that guy was passing comments on me as like that I was the only girl in that room. He was really a sweet guy. His smile was very alluring. But till now I am unable to understand why he started to fumble when I myself went there to propose him? Really! Boys are good in proposing girls but when they get themselves proposed by girls and especially in public, they feel confused. I think, he was in a confused state as he was unable to determine whether it was a real proposal or a dummy proposal. Whatever be the case, from the first day I became the face of my college which most of the students dream of!

Today when I am sitting here in this dingy cell where my life would meet its unfateful end but my soul will get its desired beginning or better say its end from these worldly affairs. But how can I say that my soul will get its end? Just because of these morons who had labelled me as a wicked, dangerous, cunning girl who had became a case study for this entire crime world. No! No! I had been a cheerful girl from the day I had taken birth and I would remain a bubbly girl till my last breath. Even in that damn college which had been the only evidence of my turmoil was once an epitome of my cheerfulness and naughtiness. That was the day when we all the four girls from the first day even before attending the first class of our college had decided to form a gang which would not only be the best gang in studies but also in fun and pranks. Oh! How much that sweet fight was when we were quarrelling over just to give that gang a suitable name for more than two hours? And finally that bamboo Shweta suggested the 'Superpower Gang' which was perhaps the suitable name seeing our enthusiasm and vigour. Without wasting a second we decided to keep that name permanent from that day only. We exploded the classroom on the very first day by uploading an adult song in one girl's mobile secretly and giving it a ring in due course of the class. What a situation it was to see her blushed face in front of the whole class!

How could we have gave our immense laughter a halt when such type of collective joy is only accessible when you get an access to a jackpot and for the time being it was not less than a jackpot. Even the teacher was literally fainted hearing an adult song from a girl's mobile. We all were seeing her through corner of the eyes as we all know that the real fun was remaining which was going to happen in the hostel. As the class got over our gang was only shouting C-Vol. 1 in the hostel and that girl was unable to catch the real culprit.

If it would have been the end of our mischief then the whole college would have forgotten it, but we made some plan for each and every one. It was now a common phenomenon to get the so called shocking situation for any guy or girl or the faculty as we would consider our target just by random selection. How can I forget the playing of a condom Ad when the Advertisement Marketing faculty was going to show us some specimens of advertisements through his ppt slide?

The whole class started to fear from this Superpower gang as no one was able to predict their next target.

Chapter-5

✤ ✤ ✤

Who says that only wicked and naughty boys get the transformation just due to a girl? I think the scholars or philosophers who gave this statement had no idea about a girl's feeling and no knowledge about a girl's heart. Perhaps that scholar would have surely been a hardcore woman who would have just felt the love of an extra wicked boy who would have fallen in love with her just because of her beauty. Who would have thought even in his wildest dreams that this extra naughty and bubbly girl whose first priority is to play pranks one day would be transformed in just a single day?

We were in the UG-3 Section of our college and life was going in a perfectly perfect way. Then one morning when we went to the college we were exclaimed to see the sudden increase in the class population. After the initial inquiry about this sudden outburst we found that one section called UG-6 had been merged with this batch as it had sparse population. Whatever be the reasons it was none of our business. We were happy as we had found the new customers for our business. Obviously we were management students and we would always think extra population as customers whether it would be a hardcore business or our pranks business.

But perhaps this population had come to close down our business. It was not the case that they were smarter than us in playing pranks or they had played a master prank on us. Being the leader of that gang I myself decided to close this gang forever. How can I forget that hot conversation which was happening in our room in the midnight at 11O' clock?

"Yar! Niharika, why do you want to close this gang?" Jasmine broke the ice after the sudden shock spread in the whole room after this declaration.

"Yes! Nihu. What's the problem? Had anyone said you anything or are you over with your pranks." Shweta also fired her arguments in a row.

"Girls, it's not like that. It is not good to make fun of everyone everytime."

"OhO! You are saying like that. I can't believe my ears." Once again Jasmine passed a counter-attack.

"Ok! Then you should believe your ears. If you don't want to stop this gang, you can operate but I am withdrawing myself from this gang."

"Nihu! We can't operate without you and you know this thing better. You are the Master-Mind behind all our operations. It can't be possible without you." Both girls were horribly sad realising the fact that when once Niharika had decided it is hard to change her decision.

"I know the reasons behind closing this gang." Anshu said in a low voice fearing any mood change of these girls.

"Then tell na, idiot!" Both girls shouted in unison.

"If I am not wrong, our Nihu had started to like any guy and she don't want to ruin her image as we all know that any student whether a boy or a girl even fear to talk with us. And the reason is quite obvious; they have not the dare to put their head in a lion's den."

"Reallyyy! Who is that lucky guy? Tell na! Nihu! Please tell na! Please..." Both girl started to question her continuously without giving time.

"It's not like that. This witch is telling a lie."

"Then tell us the truth na baby!" All girls were eager to know the name of that guy who had stolen their leader's heart.

Oh! What an awesome feeling it was to describe the quality of that guy in a total blushed state as I was not able to decide what should I tell to them and what not to tell? It was not the case that I didn't want to tell them but how could I tell them more when I myself had seen him for the first time and I was dying to talk to him as I couldn't resist myself. The only relief was that I came to know his lovely name. Oh! How sweet that name was!**'Mohit Chandra'**. I was really impressed towards his name. How much perfect his name was which was quite synonymous to his personality. He had something which made me weak or better say compel to initiate the friendship with him. But how can I say that I initiated the friendship when that day even due to heavy protest I had closed the gang practically but it was running on paper.

Chapter-6

❀ ❀ ❀

"Hii… My name is Niharika and what is your name? Will you do friendship with me?"

"Excuse me! Can I lend your pen drive as my pen drive is out of order?"

"What is the next subject in the next period?"

"One of my group member is ill, so can you please be our team member as this is very important presentation."

"Jasmine! If you will sit at that place, I will kill you. You know that is my seat."

Today when I remember those conversations, I feel what should I feel? Should I be ashamed of my choice or should I feel pity on myself that I was mad behind such a boy who is the reason of my present catastrophe. But you are saying these words today. You were feeling a sense of excitement and vigour when you were behind that rascal. But what could I do? Had I known that he would be the reason of my destruction, I would have never loved him. But my God! Tell me what was my fault that he ditched me in such a manner that no one can ditch anyone? I was insane for him in such a way that I didn't cared about my image and was crazy enough to get his love. Even behaving like a school-girl in front of him was giving me a sense of ecstasy. Today those conversations which gradually paved the way for friendship with him seems like that those were the cursed lines of any big saint who willingly cursed me so that I can lose everything in my life. My parents used to say that I am a stupid girl but hardly had I cared. Even this poor Jasmine once told me to stop behaving like a fool as I was so much immersed in his love that my every idiotic activities seemed perfect to me at that time. It was you Niharika who was proud of sticking to your decision and now when you have stucked why you are feeling pity on yourself? No! No! I am not feeling pity on myself. Why I will feel pity on myself? I am not the culprit. That damn Mohit had done all the waste activities and today this world is blaming me. Even though today I hate him from the core of my heart, but there was a time when I used to adore him, I used to love him in a way no one can love anyone.

Chapter-7

❀   ❀   ❀

What a personality that crook had got? His personality was so much adorable that even the angel of heaven would have been impressed. His well-muscular athletic body added with an impressive height of 5feet 10 Inches was enough to rise sensation in the heart of girls. His fair complexion with brown eyes was such a magic-spell that every girl would wish to immerse in that eyes forever. His dressing sense was so much adorable that every dress would feel itself privileged when he used to wear them. People say that a particular hair and beard style are suited on a particular person but Mohit was perhaps an exception. Whether he used to have clean shave or trimmed beard or long hairs or short hairs that crook was equally dashing. What a magical voice he had got? It was his sad song on the eve of the fresher party which made me insane regarding him. The way of uttering each and every word with perfect emotion and rhythm was enough to steal any girl's heart then what can I say about myself. But perhaps had I even the slightest idea that due to this moron my life would not be less than the best sad song of the world, I would have never cared about him.

What should I have done? He was a guy who was synonymous to perfection and it's the heartiest wish of any girl that her lover, her would-be husband should be perfect in everything. People use to say that it is very hard to find a rare combination of beauty with brain but I was feeling myself on the seventh sky when I used to think about him as he was the perfect combination a boy could be. He belonged from the same state from where I had came to this distant land. It was not like a typical fiction that he belonged from a poor family that I used to console my heart saying that I got attracted towards him feeling pity on him.

How can I forget that disgusting smile which he passed on me bluntly after we both were adjudged the best girl and boy respectively? But why you are thinking these things now? You were filled with excitement and inner happiness so much at that time that you had spent almost two hours describing that moment to your friends in the hostel like a daft. How much cursed I am! I had been using the sweetest, cutest, lovely and a lot more adjectives for that smile which was the beginning of my cursed life. Why God Why? People say that every event casts a shadow before its arrival, then where were You when this event was getting ready to come in my life. People say that behind every sweet smile lies the deepest grief but why you even didn't give me an omen that behind your damn sweet smile lies a black heart which will ruin my life in such a way that I haven't dreamt even in my dreams.

Chapter-8

❦ ❦ ❦

17th January; 11:30 A.M; Friday

"Hey Nihu Baby! Where are you?" Jasmine voice was full of excitement and vigour.

"Why are you so much excited? What happened?" Niharika was unable to judge the reason of this over-excitement on her friend's face.

"Today I have become no. 1 in my whole gang. This time I have left you behind...." She was speaking continuously without even taking a pause. And before Niharika could think anything further she clasped her tightly and planted a kiss on both of her cheeks.

Niharika was in a total awkward state as she was not getting any clue of Jasmine's sudden behaviour. She was in a state of pleasant surprise as she had seen her friend so much happy for the first time since she had met her.

"Jasmine! Why are you making puzzles? Tell na!" She was trying to unearth the piece of news which made her belle a mie almost insane.

"Nihu! I am in love. I am in love…." And before she could complete her sentence the whole room was covered with Niharika sudden expression and exclamation which one could expect only from girls as it normally happens to them when they hear such type of news.

"Who is that lucky guy?" After seizing her happiness and reaction she had finally bothered to ask the name of the guy.

"No! I am not going to tell you the name baby! You will yourself see him when I will return in the evening after a date with him…." Listening the word that Jasmine is also going on a date with her prince-charming she was once again insane with excitement as she couldn't even imagine that Jasmine can also go on a date. The biggest surprise or you could better say the irony was that she had told everything about Mohit and she even hasn't the slightest idea of Jasmine's love-life. She has got this auspicious news when both are going on their first date. Wondering that Jasmine never told her anything about her love; should she feel sad or envious she was not able to judge her own emotions. Obviously everyone has the right to tell what they want you to tell and what not to tell. And with mixed emotions in her heart Niharika wished her good luck for her first date. But perhaps Jasmine had sensed the feeling of despair which was rising in her friend's mind and heart at the same time. In a fraction of second she thought something which would not only handle the situation but also make her friend lively and she wouldn't feel that she had been treated as stranger.

"Nihu! I can't go on first date without you. I am feeling afraid."

As Jasmine had expected her friend passed an old excuse for not coming with her. God knows was there something reality in her sentence that she was feeling afraid or she didn't want to hurt her friend's sentiments that prompted her to make her friend ready to go with her at a' tout prix. After few minutes of false pretence from Niharika and asking for forgiveness from Jasmine that she should have told her before; the false anger of Niharika melt away and she was ready to go on the condition that Jasmine is going to give her a good treat before going there.

01:30 P.M

If everything would have been so simple, this life would have never been called life. Everyone knows that life is synonymous to unexpected circumstances and situations. At the time when both friends were rejoicing of this auspicious moment and planning what to wear and what to do for this special moment, Jasmine got a call from her father that they are about to reach station in an hour and she could come to receive her parents if she wished. Now it is not necessary to explain what would have been the thought-process of both girls at that time. Should they be happy for the gloria in excelis that Jasmine parents are coming to meet them or should they curse Him that can't He delay her parent's arrival for just a single day. Why God can be so merciless that He always brutally murders the joyful moment of anyone's life at the time when it is most needed. Can't He see that how much I was happy after getting the proposal of that boy for whom I had crush from the very first day I came to the college? But why He will give me happiness in my life? But No! The God always will give happiness to the crooked girls. When I was miserable finding that Niharika even being so much crazy about Mohit had not been even able to get a sweet smile from him, I thought that at least I am lucky that I had got my love even being less crazy than her. But as it had been said that good people are always on the mercy of god; we both are on the mercy of this unfateful god. On one side Niharika is dying to get the love of Mohit and on the other side I will be accused of telling a lie to him on the very first day of our relationship. And that's the reason boys do not trust on girls. They are right. How can anyone trust when you will break your promise on the first day? Who will make them understand that not only this damn society but also this holy shit or what we say God in the language of cultured people is the biggest enemy of girls. What could I say about my parents who can't even inform me in advance that they are coming to meet me? God knows what they think about themselves, they had said that I can come to receive them if I wish as like if I will not go to receive them they will not come to meet me. Can't they understand a simple fact that I have also something personal which I have to manage and their this sudden intruder like behaviour ruins the whole mood and occasions? Who had said them that go and meet your daughter without informing her? They say that they trust me very much. It's all bullshit. Today I have come to know at least that even my own parents don't trust me otherwise they would have informed me in advance. Let them come and see my false happiness. How I will confront him when he will meet me the next day in the class? What will I say to him? What will he think of me? God damn it! Why it happens only with me? What a fucking life I had got!

Oh! How much pure the teenage love is? Our own parents and God himself seems like our deadliest enemies when we are unable to fulfil our promise to our sweetheart due to them. Who would have thought at that time that these girls who are so much honest to their love would once get into the dungeon just due to their honesty towards their so called prince-charming!!

Chapter-9

❋ ❋ ❋

Goa; 23rd Jan; 04:00 PM; Thursday

What's the use of coming to such a place which is claimed so much romantic and sitting idle? But what can I do to make my crush a real love? People say that Goa is the sanctum sanctorum for lovers where romanticism is present in its every bit of the atmosphere but why God is not creating such an atmosphere that my dear Mohit would come and hold my hands and we would take a stroll together on the beach. What a pious feeling it would be when I would be holding the hands of my would-be husband. Then these girls would really feel jealous when they would find that a girl from a small city had been able to win the heart of the most eligible garcon of this **Symbiosis University**. Not only these girls would feel jealous but my own roommates would also feel envious when they would find that I have been able to make the beau garcon as my sweetheart. I know that they do not show their feeling directly regarding him but that **Bamboo** and **Double Battery** have a silent crush on him. These girls are really mean. Oh! How sweet it would be when I would go from here and the students will find that both of the best students of the fresher party had become the best couple of the university.

Niharika! But what do you think that Mohit would come into your room in this damn hotel and say to you that 'Please Nihu! Can we go on a date?' I know it can't happen. I know it's' an ex parte love but the con amore from my side is not worthy of rejection. What can I do? I am unable to figure out that why I am so much dumb that even being a girl I am not able to impress or better say seduce a guy whom I love from the core of my heart. Perhaps I would be the only unlucky charmante of this universe who have not even so much know-how that she can put a guy under the charm of her beauty. But what should I do, I am really not getting an idea. Think Niharika! Think. If I go on the beach wearing these absurd short-costumes, he will take me just as another who feel untrammelled when they come to any tour. But if I wear the traditional costumes which is irrelevant at this exotic place and it might happen that he may take me as **'Behan Ji'** type. No! No! I will not wear traditional costumes. Then what should I do? Think Niharika! Think. If I wear semi-casual dress with proper etiquette and sitting silently on the beach then perhaps this magic could work as it's the nature of boys that they normally get attracted towards those girls who are sitting lonely at any party or function.

"Nihu! Are you not ready yet?" Jasmine intervention broke her thought-process.

"No! No! I am ready."

"What?? Have you goanna mad? You are in the clothes which you are wearing from the morning and without changing clothes you are saying that you are ready."

Then only Niharika came into her senses and found that she is in her previous attire and her friend is looking damn hot as she had put almost the costumes which would otherwise be not perfect for any place but it was perfectly perfect for this exotic heaven.

"Oh! Sorry! Sorry! I was thinking something else."

"I know. You would have been thinking ways to impress Mohit."

"I don't want to impress him. I want to seduce him in front of my beauty. He is only mine. Only Niharika and Mohit."

"Hahaha… By the help of these damn clothes. He will not even give an imprecate look to you."

"Jasmine, you are really wicked. I am just changing clothes na. Why you are teasing me? Wait and watch."

And when Niharika came outside after five remainders and few teasing from Jasmine; even Jasmine was literally shocked to see the nulli secun dus beauty of her friend. Jasmine got so much hypnotised that she couldn't encumber herself from kissing on her friend's cheeks. Jasmine had the perfect reason to kiss her friend.

Luckily Jasmine was a girl and she had just kissed her. If there would have been a boy at that place, what would he have done it doesn't need explanations. From toe to hair, she was looking like an angel. Her well-washed hair which she had very carefully left open even after giving shape by the help of comb was adding a heavenly pleasure to the whole room. Her light make-up which was perfect seeing the moist environment was enough to mesmerize anyone's heart. These were the things which she had been gifted naturally and they were just a part of her unparalleled beauty. For the first time even the subject of kalology would have felt the scarcity of adjectives to describe her beauty. Her newly purchased blue-denim **Guess** jeans with a white full sleeve **UCB** shirt folded up to her elbows was adding a different edge to her personality. How can anyone encumber himself from being mesmerized when her soft hands were looking more elegant when she put a beautiful wrist-watch in her right hand and a bracelet in her left hand added with beautiful polished nails? Even her flat slippers were giving a meaning to her personality. How could anyone think that a girl would never wear an ornament and especially when she is getting dressed for any particular occasion? Niharika being not obsessive towards ornament had put down the appropriate ornaments which would suit her personality. Even Jasmine was surprised to see the collection of Niharika as these were the ornaments which even Jasmine was herself seeing for the first time in all these days. Her small but fabulous blue ear-rings with a thin golden chain having a cross was adding a thundering sense to this diva.

"OMG! Today only God knows how many boys will get a heart-attack. And what will happen with Mohit, I think even God would not be able to figure out."

These were the first sentence which Jasmine could utter after regaining her sense after the kissing incident.

"Jasmine! It's not like that. You know I am desperate about Mohit but I don't know what to do."

"Today he will surely propose you."

"Hey! Leave it. Don't dream in daylight. I will be happy even in this trip I will be able to have friendship with him."

"It will happen. Ok! Come."

"No! You go. I will not come."

"Why??"

"I have something in my mind."

"Whattt??" Jasmine was unable to figure out that what was running in her friend's mind as she had dressed herself in the best way and now she does not want to go on the beach. And she was more eager as she was already late.

"I am not coming." It was Niharika's final verdict.

"Ok! Do as you wish. I know you are planning something. What is the plan Nihu?"

"Chill baby! You just go and then follow the principle of 'Wait and Watch'.

And with mixed emotions in her mind Jasmine went from there.

***

"Hey Niharika! Why are you sitting alone and where is Jasmine?"

Mohit couldn't resist himself to ask something from her as he was noticing that she was sitting silently for the last one hour. He was wondering at the reason for the dullness of this cheerful face when even the dull faces were glittering. But hardly even Mohit would have an idea that it was all the by-product of Niharika sharp mind who had decided to remain a silent beauty on the beach in spite of flocking here and there. As according to her estimations and predictions a boy gets normally attracted towards a silent beauty swiftly rather than a flocking beauty. Since this time favour was in her favour and her time consumed in dressing herself had finally brought the desired results. As now Mohit had come himself to talk with her, she was on the seventh sky. But at the same time she was cautiously selecting each and every word as she can figure out the importance of this situation. And after a string of conversation, they were walking together on the beach. It was not like any Bollywood movie that they were walking together with hands in each other's neck but at least she was able to sow the first seeds of her friendship with him.

And when Jasmine eyes felt on both of them, her eyes were wide-opened with surprise.

***

"Nihu! Congrats! Best of luck for my would-be brother-in-law."

"Thank you! Thank You!"

"What magic wand had you spread upon him that he was walking with you on the beach?" Till now Jasmine was not able to understand that how it became possible.

"Jasmine baby! Silent beauty is better than flocking beauty." She said these words having a slight hint towards her dress.

"OhO! You are very intelligent." She was still confused.

"I am! Everything is fair in love and war." Her excitement was beyond expectations.

"You will never change…"

"Yep! I will never change. Never! Never!!!!"

Chapter-10

❈ ❈ ❈

What a deadly creature this examination is! Examination is such a ghost that haunts its prey in such a manner that one's whole mind gets blocked and he starts to think only about examination. He forgets all the types of enmity and friendship which he had nurtured since the last six months. The terror of this deadly ghost is to such an extent that he not only forgets everything but also fails to notice that things for which he was crazy earlier. Even Niharika and Jasmine were not an exception. Here this side the bad luck had turned its evil eyes on Jasmine. Firstly her parents had ruined her highly awaited date with her prince-charming and she had enjoyed the trip of Goa with a fake smile. Her tedious efforts didn't bore its fruit even in Goa and she was accused of betraying him as she was unable to justify her veracity. This side the very next day before she can loose the burden of her bad fate which continued even in Goa, she found a notice displaying the onset of examination in just seven days. It was needless to say that the whole college was in a panic state as everyone knows exams are exams. If it would have been a normal exam they would have some relief but this exams was different for them. It was not the case that the university was going to conduct the exams on a stricter note this time but the fact was that it was their so called first semester exams. They had the pressure of proving not only in the eyes of class and faculties but also in the eyes of their parents. It is a well-known fact that most of the undergraduate management students either come here by denying their parents' wish of pursuing engineering or medical or they had been the backbenchers in their 12th who haven't got seat in any prestigious institutions and that were their main headache. On their result of their examinations, their further pocket-money was dependent and for some of the unlucky students their love-life was dependent on this examination. And adding to the bad luck of Niharika she was in both of the category.

People had heard a lot of tales about the engineering students and the way they tackle their ghost of examination but perhaps people have been ignorant about the tales of the management students. These management students are taught to manage the company but our dear future managers utilise this knowledge how to manage their studies and exams without studying. They use the motivational and inspirational quotes for patting their back in case they are unable to get good marks. The case study which they are taught after every chapter is used in assessing the reason of their recent failure in getting good marks. They are taught the practical use of ppt that how can they summarize and explain a very important aspect at the same time and these are utilized how to make cheating materials in the form of ppt so that they can get the maximum syllabus covered in the smallest piece of paper. They not only devise smart ways of cheating which people have unheard before but also devise new motivational quotes themselves to get scot-free in case they are caught while cheating. Perhaps this would be the only course in which students arrange a fabulous party among themselves in case the whole group gets even a single back paper in their semester exams. And this side the whole department was busy in framing new authentic ways of cheating and their **SWOT Analysis** of getting all clear in the exams. Different-different papers were a fonte di tesione for different types of students. This side Accounts paper were like a mountain to climb for the science background students and the QT paper was like getting into hot water for the commerce background students. Now the time had came to test the authenticity of their friendship as willingly or unwillingly each and every group or better say gang have both type of students.

And this side Niharika was facing the so called **'Pisaach of pressure'** as she was the only the highly acclaimed JEE Rank holder in the whole UG department and at the same time she was the Ragging Queen of her class. Even the faculties were expecting her to be the college topper and she was not getting any clue even how to get pass in the examinations. The time was running like Ussain Bolt and she had not read the whole chapters even once.

This time she couldn't ask help even from Jasmine as her two papers had already gone bad. As this was not any prank that she would have ample time before executing it. She was trying to console herself by pondering upon the hardcore reality that almost every student was almost in the same situation. The only piece of contentment was that her Accounts paper had gone better than her expectation as she had prepared herself for the worst. In this game of devising new words like expectations, consolations, average and a hell lot of words through which they can motivate themselves and their friends their rest exam got over and their future went into the hands of those faculties which were a source of entertainment and pranks during the whole semester. And after arranging a consolation party the Superpower Gang headed to their respective homes.

Chapter-11

❋ ❋ ❋

Jasmine had really said that I will never change. I know that I will not change, but who am I to force my attitude and thought-process on any other person? Today this girl whose name is not only Jasmine but is also as sweet and fragrant as jasmine had been trapped into this cobweb which had been created by me whether it be unwillingly or willingly. Who am I to ruin the life of this girl who had not dreamt even in her dreams that she would have to pay a hefty price for befriending with me? No! Niharika No! She is not paying a price for befriending with you. If it would have been the case your every friend should have been here but to your sad demise; no one is here. It's not the price but its' her genuine character and nice upbringing which had made her not to leave you in the en route when the whole world was against you. Really she is a girl having a very genuine character who has fulfilled her each and every promise till ad extremum. And I am not saying this because she is with me here in this hell. Even when she met me for the first time in the college she had been true to her words. Whether it be giving a party or completing your assignment she had never gone against her words. It was the charm of her sharing attitude that used to tempt any girl or a boy equally to have friendship with him. But one thing which was really remarkable about her was that she had a very crystal clear understanding of the fact who wants to have a genuine friendship with her and who wants to take the advantage of her lavish lifestyle. It was her kindness and compassionate behaviour which made her apart from the other rich kids who always went through the campus flaunting their parent's wealth. I was normally repulsive towards these rich kids but her nature of helping everyone whether he be the peon or the faculty had attracted me towards her and perhaps the decision of befriending with her would remain the best decision of my this short-span life. Oh! How much ungrateful I am that I am returning the gifts of her friendship with a death penalty to her? Why God Why?

Chapter-12

❋ ❋ ❋

What a moment it was for all of us! Every student in the hostel was preparing to go back to his home after our highly tensed phase of exam had got over. How can I miss those moments even today when each and every creature of the hostel was trying to get back at its previous as there were very fair chances of being caught? If there would have been a good observer she would have got the full entertainment and that even free of cost. A lot of girls are trying to make understand that even though they love their prince-charming very much but why they can't talk to them after reaching their original destination. The reasons given by them were like the best jokes cracked by any excellent stand-up comedian. Someone is making a dry face as her younger brother or sister sleeps in the same room and some other are making hue and cry as they will be not allowed to talk on phone once they would reach their respective homes. What a funny scene it was when I heard one girl that she is forbidding her sweetheart as her sister-in-law would tease her if she would get to know that she had made a boyfriend? Few were hanging fire either due to their strict father or their spy natured mother who is in the habit of digging each and every thing about their daughters. The funniest conversation that was happening in my own room between that "Bamboo" and "Double Battery". That Double Battery was asking to Bamboo how will she manage her earlier two boyfriends now when she would reach there as till now she had managed by asking them not to spend much money on phone as they have to make STD calls. What a people they are who had made love as time-pass?

Beside this love game a lot of such things were happening at that time which would have been a source of nice observation. Everyone was inquiring about the railway timings and the list of various trains such that they had set up here the railway headquarters of Indian Railways. Someone is trying to purchase gifts for their family members and others are purchasing decent clothes for them. But the most thrilling scene was having a view of deleting the so called hot songs and videos from their laptops and mobiles as they were the so called 'Good Daughters' of their parents.

Beside these entertainments I was myself in a somewhat tensed situation as for the first time in my life I was going back to my own home. I was almost in an egarement situation that what to carry and what not to carry to home. After few suggestions from Jasmine and applying my mother wit I headed to my own home saying good-bye to my gang. But my all tension and awkwardness disappeared when I got a warm welcome from my parents. I could understand that they were very happy as they were seeing their daughter after almost six months. As it has been said that surprises are like prizes but how can anyone ponder on these thoughts before a simple girl like me would find herself being treated like a princess between her friends. I was greeted with open arms even by those friends who barely deserved to be called my friend as they were not in my friend circle. Everyone was trying to know about my college, the city and a hell lot of things. Everyone was listening to me so attentively that I was myself in a shocked state that what had happened to them? These are the girls who were once eager to say their own part but now they are feeling themselves on the seventh sky when they are listening my stories as it would have been their own story. For the first time in my life I was getting a very warm treatment from my every near and dear ones. It seemed like everyone is fraught to become the part of my story. But alas! They would become a character of my story in such a way; even I hadn't dreamt of? How much a person is desperate to tell her own story, I had sadly enjoyed that day when my one friend asked me about my any love story and rebuked me on a friendlier tone for not collecting enough courage even to propose my own prince-charming. How much I had talked about that malignant crook and the way I was describing his each and every quality; even the greatest poets would have found a sense of complexion in describing the beauty of a person? How much ungrateful

I was that I was busy in declaring him as the best guy of this universe who had been the reason of this present catastrophe? How could I have been so much wrong even I can't understand? You are telling these things now but at that time you were feeling a sense of pride while narrating his story. You were feeling a sense of ecstasy when all your friend were informed by that girl and all were teasing you for your that so called prince charming. How much ungrateful I was? I was asking suggestions and tips from them that how should I propose them or better say how can I invite the impending disaster in my life as soon as possible. But you were the girl who had a single motive in her mind that was only and only how to hit the nail on the head as you didn't want to invite the possibility of being ignored by him due to any silly reasons. You were the girl who after taking the so called tricks and techniques from your friend circle to make him your own soulmate; you headed back towards the university.

Chapter-13

❀ ❀ ❀

Whatever be the case today that Niharika Ahuja is today going to get an almost sure shot death penalty and her best friend Jasmine is an equal partner of the crime but had anyone met Niharika that time he would have found out a different Niharika. At that time Niharika had only one and one motive in her mind and undoubtedly this was to get the love of Mohit Chandra. She was so much focussed towards Mohit Chandra that even the Arjun of Mahabharata would have felt inferiority complexion regarding his focus. God knows what she had felt towards Mohit that 24*7 only one name was revolving in her mind. After the incident of Goa where she had got the initial success her heart was bouncing and bouncing. Even the Olympic Gold medallist would have not been so much happy as she had been after that incident. It is right that that today she is oscillating between nice thoughts and bad feelings continuously but there was a time when she was an etranger to tension and worries. Why would she be sad or in tension when she was able to get the opportunity to talk with that guy in private for whom she was desperate from the day she had seen him?

She was feeling herself on the seventh sky when she found that her Mohit is talking to her continuously from that day without any break. As soon as this fact glanced in her mind suddenly she was feeling herself the most blessed girl of this universe. And as she was instantaneous in taking any decision she decided promptly to propose him. Her this instantaneous decision was not only due to the fact that the idea of proposing her erupted suddenly. When few days before she was in her home city her friend's satire for not getting enough courage to propose a boy ignited the spark and being honest it provided a solid reason for her sudden decision. But her one thought said her that at least she should share this awesome piece of news to Jasmine that she was going to propose him as she was the only girl whom she used to trust fully in this university. Had anyone listened that conversation at that time they would have wondered why this catfight is happening? But they were Jasmine and Niharika; they were just like that.

***

"Jasmine! Come here. I want to tell you something." Niharika was her at the top of voice.

"What happened? Has Mohit proposed you that you are so much happy?" Jasmine teased her to get some fun from her extra excitement.

"No re! I am going to propose him tomorrow."

"Whattt??? Don't you think that its' so early?" Her mouth remained opened after the sudden announcement of Niharika.

"You know na, I am a fast girl. And you know after that day we have been talking regularly." Niharika was putting emphasis on each and every word of the second line.

"But, if…." Jasmine was not even able to complete her sentence and she interrupted.

"I am going to propose him tomorrow and that's final." She said in an assertive tone as she could not bear the fact that anyone would throw cold water on her regarding Mohit; even Jasmine.

"Nihu! Listen me. If you want to propose him then why don't you propose him on 14ᵗʰ Feb? It's the day for true lovers and it's also just day after tomorrow. Can't you wait for one more day?"

"Oho! How much stupid I am? I boast that I love my Mohit truly and even don't know that which is the pious day for true lovers?"

Had Jasmine had given any other reason to delay the day of her proposal she would have never accepted but it was the charm of the words of 'true lovers' used by Jasmine that not only she accepted her suggestion but also gave her a party in the nearby restaurant for giving her such a brilliant idea. How much rigorously her that day went in firstly declaring her stupid as why she didn't had such a brilliant idea as her one stupidity could have made her apart from Mohit. And the rest of the day of both friends went in planning and rehearsing how to propose her prince-charming.

Chapter-14

❋ ❋ ❋

14th February; Friday

Today is 14th February. People say it is called 'The Valentine Day'. The day which had been specially made for the true lovers. The day when couples go on a date, kiss and hug each other. But what should I say about my imprecate luck when today each and every couple had made their plans for outing, I am entangled in my own cobwebs. What should I do? Should I propose him directly or should I do something extra? What would happen if I propose him directly and he would take me as an unromantic girl? But it may also happen that if I would try to do something extra and this precious moment get lost then I will not forgive myself for being labelled as oversmart. What a foolish girl I am that I have not even the basic know-how to propose a boy whom I love from the core of my heart? You know Niharika, even though how much you boast of being fast there is always a fly in your ointment. You had already missed one chance of proposing him on the eve of Propose Day and now you are crying over the split milk. No! No! I am not crying on the split milk and neither have I missed the chance. I don't want to cut a sorry figure of myself on this day. What would have been the difference when I would have also proposed him on the Propose Day as all other girls do? But the basic problem is that how would I say to him that I love him and he would have enough trust on my love that he would accept my love whole-heartedly. Nihu! Its only 12:30 in the morning and you have enough time to make a plan or better say to think upon how to create an atmosphere which would not only mesmerize him but also make him feel that you are the best girl for him.

Oh! How much pure and desperate the teenage love is? A guy or a girl do not wake up even at 8O' clock in the morning when the exam is at 9O'clock but they are awake at the midnight morning so that they do not even lose a single second of this auspicious day. The parents and the so called intelligentsia group can advocate that our young generation is going on the wrong path. But perhaps if they would have lend their thought-process even for a single second on their pious love they would have felt proud on the same young generation for respecting this pious virtue. Even though a teenager is aware of the fact that he could ruin his career and get in trouble but how will he justify himself in the court of the Almighty when his own life would be in a permanent setback due to his own negligence towards his beloved?

And Niharika who was the star performer in planning for the first time was unable to turn the corner but after an hour of exercise to her 18gm (brain) she set herself for this auspicious day and went again to bed.

***

She got up from her bed in a very relaxed mood at 9 O'cock. Even Jasmine and her other roommates were astonished to see the expression on Niharika face as everyone had assumed that she would be in a very panic state as this was perhaps the most important day in her life. On the contrary her posture and expression were telling a different tale. She was in pace like an l'allegro. Jasmine couldn't resist herself from asking that had Mohit had proposed her that she in such a relaxed state? But getting a non-affirmative answer was enough to make their mouth wide-opened in exclamation. The whole Super gang was aware of the fact that once again their leader had made a master plan and it was better for them to obey the traditional philosophy of 'Wait and Watch.'

Niharika started the expedition by making a call to Mohit and making him agree for meeting in a nearby mall so that they can start this day with an awesome movie and further planning according to situation. As per their gang's estimation she put on the same dress which made her labelled as silent beauty. And seeing her costume Jasmine said something which made the atmosphere lively for a moment as each and everyone in the room was watching her each and every move.

"Nihu Baby! How the Silent Beauty would propose her beloved as she is going to be silent for the whole day?"

Niharika didn't reply her and just passed a smile towards her.

And when Niharika was about to leave with a sans souci on her face, everyone wished her good luck and put a demand for party in the evening which one could except from the friends.

***

What a coincidence it was that for the first time neither of them has to wait as both reached on the decided time almost together. Finally after a formal greeting they headed towards the multiplex. God knows why Niharika had selected to watch a movie with Mohit today? Here her friends were wondering that what their leader was going to do today and on the other side Mohit even chewing the cud for a long time was not able to figure out the reasons. He knew that she loves her but what of kind of love; it was beyond his assessment capacity. He wondered that it might happen that she wants to steal the show by initiating some erotic activities so that he can feel how much she loves him? But nothing was happening. She was busy in watching movie. It was not the case that it was any blockbuster movie that would let the spectators mesmerized but she was intact in her activities.

If anyone would have seen her from a bird's eye view he would have thought the same thing. But the reality was that after each and every moment Niharika was getting nervous and was trying hard to look normal. Her mind was engrossed in minding her own P's and Q's of this dies faustus. She was trying to pacify herself by several thoughts but the desired fruit were miles away. Even she had planned all the things carefully but it seemed to her that she was missing the mark. It was like a typical situation that they are in a movie theatre as they are on any specified date. It was not the case that the normal thoughts of being reading his mind or the fear of getting rejected were erupting in her head at the time movie was playing on the screen. As it was an open secret that she loved him very much; she was damn sure about her love and she was genetically confident. When the best of the beaux a prits and preux chevaliers start to tremble at this juncture she was just a teenager and even though she was trying to keep calm; time was hanging heavy in her hands as she was unable to put herself in the driving seat. This side Mohit was forecasting the next situation in which he was going to be in with her and that side Niharika was calculating the chances of getting the fruits of her extreme penance which she was following sacredly like a ritual. And how the three hours passed both were unable to assess as the 'The End' flashed on the screen.

As Mohit had forecast they went to a nearby restaurant and had their sumptuous meal. Even he was surprised that is it just the element of the surprise package or it was just like that. It was not the case that he was any magician or a priest that he would have a prescience of Niharika's plans. It was all gratitude of that Jasmine who had told her in advance that Niharika is going to propose her today and that's why he had accepted Niharika call of joining in her mall leaving the bachelor party. He was extremely surprised that now they are going to a nearby park so that they can spend the time altogether. His excitement was on the seventh sky as now it was the high time to get proposed by the most beautiful girl of the university as now she was sitting in a relaxed state so that she can propose her beloved. But Mohit was unable to determine that when she had specially chosen this day for proposing him then why she is delaying? Or had once again this Super gang had played a prank on them? Was Jasmine lying or something is obstructing her to propose him? No! No! Jasmine would not be lying. She had told me that how dearly she loves me and even I had seen this. But what is stopping her? Mohit! Are you foolish or what? She is a girl and you are a boy. You should know that girls normally do not propose upfront and added to your demise she is a small town-girl. If you would not propose yourself you will lose the best girl of this university. Even your friends will make a mockery of you when they would get to know that you had kicked upon your own ass by being arrogant. Even Jasmine had said that she was coming to propose me. What would if she is wrong? Isn't it enough for you to make surety that she has no amant and she is with you when she could be with any garcon of her choice. A ripple of fear and anxiety and god knows which type of emotions was erupting in Mohit's 18gm.

"Nihu! I have to say something." Mohit tried to deflect the normal course of the conversation.

"Tell na!"

As it could be expected from a teenager he put his hands in Niharika's hand softly with mixed emotions in his heart and tried to get away from his self-created cobweb of arrogance and tried to win her love by repeating a few love quotes initially and telling those three magical words to Niharika for which she was dying to hear from the day she had seen her beloved.

"I Love You Niharika! I love you. I love you."

"I Love You Mohit! I love you too."

And when they headed for their own destinations she was wondering that once again **'Silent Beauty had proved herself better than the flocking beauties.'**

Chapter-15

❀ ❀ ❀

After the highly awaited acceptance of her love, Niharika's life turned over a new leaf. The girl who was busy in thinking about giving his love a destination was now enjoying each and every moment of her life. How much happiness she was enjoying in her life even she was not able to assident. It seemed that she had got a jackpot. Talking continuously on the phone, going on a date on regular basis was like a ritual for her. Oh! How much sweet feeling this love is? If anyone would have asked Nihu about love she would have described the cuteness and sweetness of this virtue endlessly for hours. The scholars had rightly said that when you are in love every bit of the atmosphere seems to possess romanticism. And Niharika was not an exception. She was enjoying each and every bit of life. The girl who used to envy those girls when they used to tease her no longer got angry. She used to laugh at that comments as being her friend it were their right to tease their leader and the best couple of this universe. How much sweet this love is that a person gets transformed in a fraction of second? Now Niharika orario (time) got used to utilize her empty time schedule in planning how to make her love a life-long journey. And this virtue is on a different edge when you are in love for the first time. And when our Niharika got blessed to get this feeling she was trying hard not to commit any silly mistake which would ruin her happiness. But perhaps Niharika had not an idea that when you are going through the best phase of our life, we should not forget a very simple fact of the life that the worst phase of life can come to us and that even without warning.

Niharika unaware of these philosophical insights was riding on the ship of commitment towards her prince-charming whom she now considered her would-be-husband.

Chapter-16

❀ ❀ ❀

"Hey Nihu darling what you are going to gift your prince on his birthday?"

"Why should I tell you idiot!" Even Jasmine was enjoying in poking her friend as she knew that her friend was very possessive in nature regarding Mohit and didn't like any intervention even on a friendlier tone.

"Now I became idiot and Mohit had become cleverer." She was teasing her continuously

"It's not like that." She sensed the impending satire in her friend's tone and felt bad for not including her in this planning as Jasmine was her best friend.

"Actually I am planning to give him a very beautiful watch on his birthday." Niharika continued.

"Really Nihu! You will remain an idiot. This is his first birthday with you and it should be a dies festi for both of you. You should give him something special which will mark how much you adore him."

"Then give me any clue na."

"Go to the Barbeque Nation and arrange a solo party for him in which there would only be two names and neither of us and nor his friends." Jasmine passed a wicked smile seeing the attention of her friend whenever she used to give any suggestion regarding Mohit.

***

Really Jasmine was right. I should give him something special that would mark that how much I adore him. But would the idea of arranging a solo party for him would be right? It could be a better option but wouldn't it be so much old-fashioned that I would make a fool of myself. I know that he is so nice that he will not say anything but even though I should think something better for him. Think Niharika think! What should I do for him? Should I call him to the hostel or should I do anything else. But even I can't do that as it is a girl's hostel and boys are not allowed to enter and you are thinking to arrange a solo party for him in a girl's hostel. How it would be to go to his flat? But wouldn't it be a bad idea as there will be his friends there and they would take me as a nasty girl. Then what should I do for my would-be-husband which would not only make him glad but can prove the best gift ever on his birthday. It should be such which had not been given by anyone neither by his friends nor by his parents.

And as the word would-be-husband flashed in her mind she started to wonder about that things which is not only morally bad but also not legal. But as it has been said that there is nothing good nor bad in love. She patted herself by saying that everything is fair in love and war. And as we all know that a teenage heart is as pure as the water of the Ganges which do not care about the morality and legality once they are assured that it is going to make happy their beloved and it would make her close to her beloved. And in a fraction of second she decided to present herself as a birthday gift to her prince-charming. She decided to give her heart, her soul, her body and everything possible on his birthday as she was his soulmate. But it was not easy for her to make up her mind to give herself as a birthday gift to her amant. She was not only sensing a wave of fear that she would be taken as a cheap girl or a characterless girl but also her small town background was not allowing her conscience for this gift. If today one would had read the thought-process of Niharika then he would have understood that why the scholars always advocate that our young generation is going off the track. We teenagers feel blushed when we find that our most of the friends had lost their virginity and we are the single piece in the lot who are sticking on the old tradition. And Niharika was not an exception. Whenever her all friends used to talk about their garcons and their sex life she would feel an inferiority complex as she had not kissed her love even a single time. What's the thought-process of teenager are that they want to be no. 1 in each and every field without regarding the moral and immoral consequences of the activity. Even though she was not able to figure out as she was not still sure that is it right or wrong or what effect it would cast on her further life? But as it has been said that the effect of the wrong suggestions possess more effect on our mind than the right suggestion. Already our friend circle is notorious for giving such suggestions. 'Nothing will happen', 'No one get to know these things', 'This is the modern world', 'Change your mindset', 'Why you are acting like a loser', 'You do not have enough courage', 'You do not love her truly' are some of the nasty piece of suggestions and so called motivational quotes which force them to initiate the act of pre-marital sex. And these all the negative suggestions would not have cast an effect on Niharika but how can the friand heart of Nihu could bear that she would be blamed by her own friends not to love Mohit truly as she had not let him kiss her even. The bio-chemical imbalance which sometimes let a person think that she would also try these things compels a person to take this decision. And as Niharika was the only virgin girl in her friend-circle she decided to shade this shameful label forever and give her would-be-husband the best birthday gift of his life.

Oh! How much the world has changed? The same label of being virgin which was seen with respectful eyes had now turned as a shameful label for the teenagers. As being virgin they consider themselves outdated, idiot, foolish, unromantic and a hell lot of things which had become the source of consideration not only for the parents but also for the society.

Chapter-17

❋ ❋ ❋

17th July; 08:00 AM; Tuesday

Today it was the birthday of Mohit Chandra or better say it was the birthday of Niharika's would-be-husband. From the early morning she was so much excited as it seems that it was her birthday. She was not only busy but also in tension as she wanted to enjoy this day as much as possible and without any hassles. Her cheerfulness and bubbliness were enough to create a sense of jealousy for other girls. And why shouldn't she be happy as she had got more than what she aspired for? She had thought that they would celebrate his birthday in a restaurant and other things will be planned further but he agreed to invite her on his flat and he was about to come to take her from the hostel from where they would proceed further. She was in a relaxed state even after being in the possession of the slight degree of tension which normally happens on such type of occasions. Whenever she pondered upon the fact that she was going to his flat her joys knew no boundations. Her excitement was on a different level when she wondered how much romantic it would be when he would hold her in his arms. She was not able to gauge the level of contentment when Mohit would kiss her. Oh! How much a sweet moment it would be when we would be two body but just one soul.

"Hey! Niharika, Mohit is calling you." Jasmine came to give the phone which she had left in her room.

"Ok! Ok!" She started to stumble confronting the present.

She took the cellphone from Jasmine at once to ask for just two more minutes from him as she had to travel all along the campus to reach up to the gates. And after looking herself once again in the mirror she went from there.

***

"Wow! Mohit, you live here? Really its' a nice house." Niharika felt excited to see the grandeur of the flat once she entered the house and she couldn't hide her excitement which was crystal clear on the face of Niharika.

"Yep! It's this collection of debris where your this slave uses to hide his head." Mohit replied in a satirical tone.

"Hahaha... Always funny!"

Finally both entered into the only bedroom of that so called mansion as it was a single room flat. Niharika was astonished to see how each and every things ranging from television to sofa were beautifully decorated in that small flat. As they rested on the sofa she once again greeted him 'Happy Birthday' which was for the seventh time on this day.

"You are once again wishing me happy birthday for the seventh time."

"It's my wish how many time I wish my would-be-husband 'Happy Birthday'. And she passed a wicked smile to him.

"Ok baby! Can we celebrate our birthday with the permission of my lord?"

"Oh! Yes."

Both arranged the cake on the table to lit the candles and once again after saying him happy birthday she blew off the lighted candles. (She forgot that it was Mohit's birthday not hers.) Mohit sliced the piece of cake and both ate the first slice with each other's hand. And Mohit just kissed her on her cheeks.

"Oh no idiot!" She said in a frowned tone.

"What happened dear?" He was almost puzzled seeing her frowned tone.

"Not now idiot! We have enough time for this. Firstly I want to do something for you."

"What baby?" He was not able to assident about what she was talking about. As it is the nature of boys that if they know that they had got the privilege of kissing their beloved with her consent they become impatient.

"I want to prepare my favourite dish for you on this occasion and you go to the bathroom to get fresh."

After he came from bathroom he was astonished to see a sweet dish nicely decorated in a plate engraved "Happy Birthday Mohit Chandra" as it was engraved on the cake.

"Wow! How did it you prepared it so soon in just a matter of few minutes."

"Its' my talent baby!"

"Tell na!"

"Actually I had prepared it especially for you in the morning in the hostel and gave it a final touch in your kitchen."

"So sweet! So sweet!" He once kissed on her cheeks.

"Ok! Ok! Don't go emotional and let's eat together."

Both started to enjoy the sweet dish together which had perhaps become sweeter for Niharika as what else she would have expected from her life. Niharika was thanking her stars in her sub-conscious mind as life was going as much beautiful as she had not even dreamt of. She had the reason to be so much happy as she was the luckiest girl of the universe who was getting perhaps more love from her beloved which she had dreamt in her life. Even though she was eating she was looking straight into the eyes of Mohit and God knows what prompted her she kissed Mohit on her cheeks in the due course of the meal and Mohit got a pleasant surprise as it was least expected at this juncture of time. And as it is the nature of the boys when they get the sweetest things of the universe (A girl kiss on her initiation) they hardly care for anything else. Mohit put aside the plate from the table and kissed her on her cheeks and pulled her towards the bed.

"What are you doing Mohit?"

"Just glancing at the most beautiful girl of this universe who has given me the chance to get her precious love. I love you Nihu!"

"OhO! So funny."

He couldn't stop his bouncing heart to kiss her on her foreheads. He came over her body and put his lips on her lips. Both lips were rubbing together and Nihu was feeling a sense of ecstasy after getting the warmth of a male body for the first time. She was getting sensational with each and every second and she was losing her control.

"At least close the door baby!"

"No one is here. Relax na."

Getting assured that she is safe in his arms, she initiated the kiss as now she do not want to waste any moment. She bite the lips of Mohit as now it was almost unable to bear the exotic heat coming from other's end. And in a fraction of second both tongues were playing their part in each other's mouth. After the storm was over there was a sense of contentment on each other's face. It seemed that they have got everything in their life. How couldn't their contentment find itself on the seventh sky as everyone knows about the charm of the first kiss of their life? As it was the first kiss of Niharika which she had enjoyed with her sweetheart for whom, she was extremely passionate and careful. Even before she could think further this time Mohit initiated the kiss and once again they were in each other arms. Could this kiss end just to each other lips? Instead he was kissing all around her neck and biting her neck softly which was giving her an insane pleasure.

"What are you doing Mohit? It hurts."

"Really?"

Instead of giving her reply she bite his neck a little harder before she could hug him as tightly as possible. He started to kiss down the neck and as at this juncture clothes seems irrelevant he started to slowly unbutton her shirt.

"You are a total idiot! You don't know anything." Niharika showed a false anger.

"What happened dear?" Mohit was shocked to see the wave of anger on Niharika's face.

"Leave it! Nothing." She said in a frowned tone.

"I understood."

And after opening his second button he passed a gentle kiss on her cheeks.

"Now better."

What could she say? Instead of replying anything she passed a sweet smile to him. This whole process continued till he unbuttoned all the buttons of her shirt. Finally when she put aside her shirt Mohit couldn't believe his eyes. He was seeing her with wide eyes. What a beautiful figure she had got? Her each and every curve of the body was enough to make him spell-bound. He was feeling that either he has reached in heaven or still he is in his dreams. He was wondering when even she had just shed her shirt he is going insane, then what will happen when after few moments she will shed all her clothes. He was considering himself the luckiest guy of this universe; as for the first time in his life he had seen such an unparalleled beauty!

"What happened? Am I not looking good?" Niharika intervened her seeing the shocked state of his face.

"Good! My god; you are awesome, gorgeous, cute, seductive…."

"Ok! Ok! Stop."

Even though she had said him to stop how could he stop himself after being the sole spectator of such a seductive beauty? Even if he would try to stop which was almost impossible what could he stop he was himself still wondering? Setting all these thoughts aside he kissed on her half-covered breasts one by one and removed her bra. After that he couldn't stop himself from getting immersed into her breasts and as now Niharika was unable to resist herself she started to unbutton the shirt of Mohit and this time it was the chance of Niharika to get spell-bound. How much she had been wrong in her imagination? The athletic body of Mohit was far better than she had imagined. Muscular body having wide chests were enough to create sensation in the heart of Niharika and she was felling for the first time that her decision of presenting herself as a birthday gift is not going to prove wrong. And when both person are spell-bound by each other's body physique the charm of getting close to each other increases multiple times. Both were playing with each other's half naked body and when they put off their whole clothes none of them knew.

"OMG!" Niharika screamed confronting the present as she felt a severe pain in her vagina as the organ of Mohit had tried to penetrate her.

"Mohit! Its' paining a lot. Do something." She was moaning and crying in pain and was unable to figure out anything.

"It happens when you are for the first time." Mohit tried to console and pacify her.

But these words had a little effect on her as now it had started bleeding from her organs and the pain was unable to bear. She was literally in tears when Mohit ejected his organs out and kissed her. He cleared the stains of blood and changed the bed sheet which was there on the bed.

"Mohit! It hurts a lot." She said in despair with almost tears in her eyes again.

He wiped her tears and tried to console her and make her understand that as she is virgin it's a normal thing and there is nothing to worry.

Oh! What a scene it was when her sweetheart was making him understand the basics of a human body while they were lying naked in each other's arms. And as the time passed and as both them couldn't resist each other's closeness they once again immersed into each other. Earlier the activity which was painful for Niharika was giving her such immense pleasure which she didn't want to end forever. She was herself feeling ashamed in her sub-conscious mind for being ignorant about a girl's body. She was enjoying the charm of the athletic body of Mohit who sometimes was very soft and sometimes his each stroke was so hard that he doesn't care what was going in other's mind. But this is the human body which loves this mixture as it gives such peace and pleasure which is beyond imagination. Niharika was feeling blessed to lose her virginity with a person who loves her so much but then suddenly someone knocked the outside door.

"OMG! Mohit someone is there. What will happen now?" Niharika was almost in a panicked state.

"Dear, why are you taking tension. This is my personal flat. No one can come here without my permission."

"But baby! I am fearing a lot." The sense of despair was crystal clear on her face.

"There would be any neighbour who might have come to ask for something. Ok! I am going to see that who is there. I am with you na! Then why are you taking tension."

"Ok!"

Mohit went from there. Niharika started to find her clothes which had been scattered but before she could wear her underpants she was shocked to see that Prakash entered into the bedroom.

"OhO! You are playing love game." Prakash passed a satirical tone seeing the scene around the bedroom.

Seeing Prakash in the room Niharika was in such a despair state which needs not an explanation. She was unable to utter out a single word from her lips. The lips which had a few moments before were telling a different story went dry.

"It's not like that." Mohit tried to give the justification.

"I understand everything. I want a share or I will expose you." Prakash said in an assertive tone.

Niharika felt that someone had hit her with an iron rod. She grabbed her head with both her hands.

"Aye! Rascal. It can't be possible." Mohit said in a loud voice full with anger.

"Its' your choice baby! Either get exposed or let me have sex. Niharika, you are intelligent. Its' your choice." Prakash said in a firm tone.

Niharika was in such a shocked state that she was not able to think anything. But it was not the time to think anything. The disaster had happened and she was full of tears.

"Tell me your decision quickly. I can't wait." The tone of Prakash was commanding in nature.

"Ok!" She accepted her command as she had no option.

"That's nice. Mohit, go outside and close the door."

Mohit went from there repenting on his luck.

"Hey bitch! What you are seeing? I am not your boyfriend that I will make love to you. I will just fuck you bitch. By the way you are a sexy whore."

Niharika feeling helpless started to open her bra and panty which she had managed to wear at that time.

"Take my penis into your mouth." He commanded her

"Whattt??"

"Are you deaf? I said to take my penis into your mouth, you slut?"

Seeing no any option she took his penis into her mouth and he grabbed her long hairs and he started to fuck her mouth in a beastly manner. And when he ejaculated after few moments, he commanded her to lie on the bed and open her legs wide. She followed her instructions and he started to fuck her hardly without any emotions. And when the storm was just over she was astonished that the gate opened and Rajesh entered the bedroom.

"Oho! Prakash you are fucking such a slut and you didn't told me. I also want to enjoy the pussy of this slut." Rajesh passed his crooked smile towards Prakash.

Niharika was literally devastated to find that Rajesh was also one of Mohit's friend. And she understood the whole scenario in a fraction of second. The interruption of Prakash was not any coincidence but it was the master plan of Mohit. He had invited his friends. Her heart sank in despair that she had been betrayed by that guy whom she had considered more than her life. But what was the use of crying over spilt milk?

"Mohit! You bastard! You had betrayed me." Niharika said at the top of her voice.

Listening her voice he came inside the room and slapped her hardly. He heartlessly advised her to remain calm and serve as slave for his friends for today's night as she was their party material on his birthday. She started to cry listening his reply.

"O bitch! Keep silent and let me fuck you. And Prakash you should go outside."

"Ok!"

As soon as Prakash turned his back Rajesh started to bite her both breasts mercilessly. It was giving a lot of pain to her but this pain had been overshadowed by the pain which she had got by the betrayal of Mohit Chandra. Rajesh also fucked her mercilessly and as soon as he completed his turn Santosh came inside the room and Rajesh went from there. Now her mind had got blank and now she was wondering that how many mother-fuckers she would have to serve before this ordeal could come to an end. Santosh was at least lenient than others and he simply screwed her without any foreplay or to make her commit any nasty activities. And as soon as Santosh completed his turn Abhishek came in the room.

Now she had almost surrendered herself.

"Don't take tension. I am the last." He said in a shameless tone.

What does it matter? I have already been ruined. Who cares that you are the last or more insatiable wolves are yet to come.

"As everybody has fucked you, I will do something else. I will fuck in you a way no one would have fucked anyone."

Abhishek fucked her in the most unnatural way which was not only immoral but also a matter for shame even for a lascivious scoundrel. It was so much poignant that made her almost scream as she was unable to bear the pain. After he completed his turn he went outside and all those barbarians came into the room together.

"Long live Mohit Chandra. Happy Birthday Mohit." All of them cheered out loud in unison.

"What should we do with this slut?" Mohit asked his friends.

"Don't say her slut yar! She had given us immense pleasure." Rajesh interrupted.

Niharika was feeling that each and every word of these rogues seemed like a row of harpoons which were getting pierced in her heart one by one. She was wondering that as now she has been into a catastrophe and as this ordeal had end; she will have to be ready to face this humiliation. But poor Niharika hadn't the slightest idea that the worst was yet to come. Perhaps she had forget the basic principle of life that once the witch of bad fate catches its prey it doesn't leave her prey so much easily and in her case she was trapped in the dungeon of ordeal.

"She is the modern Draupadi of the modern Pandavas who will enjoy from her today as much as possible." Abhishek passed this statement with so much pride as he has said any philosophical quote

"Yep! The time is only 7O' clock and as Mohit had said that she will serve as slave for the whole night. And if we will leave her this time she will feel very bad. That's not good. She had made us happy and we will make her enjoy the whole night. Cheer up for today's night slave cum slut cum Mohit's sweetheart." It were the words of Santosh.

"Cheers! Long live our Mohit Chandra." All cheered once again.

"Ok! You wear your clothes and take some rest till the time we take our dinner." Mohit said to her as he was ordering her and all the friends went into the drawing room.

***

Why God Why? Why did he do this to me? What was my fault? He has torn out my soul in such a way no one had ever done this. He not only raped me but also made me rape with his lascivious gang whom he had invited so that they can fuck me. Am I a slut as they are referring me? Or a bitch who has been trapped into such a cachot from where there is no exit? What is my fault? People say that You see everything but where are you this time when I need You the most. These crooks are rejoicing at their triumph and I am sitting here lamenting on Your mercy. Please God please have some pity on me. I beg in front of you. Please let me out from this hell. Please God please. If loving anyone unconditionally is a sin then I have committed this sin but please help me. If letting anyone immersed in heart to such an extent that he becomes synonymous to your life is a mistake, I committed that mistake. But please help me. And if loving anyone from the core of one's heart is not a mistake, then tell me what my fault was? Why had he done this to me? Why God Why? If there is a god in this world, then please help me.

She was engrossed in her helpless thoughts crying for the moon and begging to Him in her sub-conscious mind, just then Mohit entered the room and slapped her hard which let her to confront the present situation where she had been trapped.

"How dare you to disobey me you bitch!" He was shouting and slapped her once again.

"What happened?" All his friends came in the bedroom and asked the reason.

"She is thinking that I am his boyfriend as earlier and she will show her false pretence and I will bear that. Listen you bitch! You are our slave and we all will now slap you two times each before you get dressed up as this is your punishment for disobeying us. Isn't it right bro…"

All replied in affirmative and started to slap her one by one and she was crying and as loud she cried the harder the next slap were. After the slapping ordeal got over she got dressed up.

"Now light the cigarettes for all of us." Mohit once again passed his order.

She unwrapped the packet of cigarette which they had brought and started to put into their mouth one by one lighting them.

"Now open your mouth!" The next order came from Prakash

And as soon she opened her mouth he blew the whole smoke into her mouth and she started to cough.

"Don't pretend and go to each and every one turn by turn."

Her hesitant thought-process got rewarded in the form of a hard slap from Prakash and she started to consume the smoke of everyone. How could these rascals who had labelled her as Modern Draupadi left her just by making her inhale the smoke of their cigarettes? They forced her to smoke three cigarettes in a row which could at least make her a modern girl in their eyes before they transform her into something different. As the time was passing their each and every activity was becoming tough for Niharika to perform. After they drank their share of wine they were not only talking rubbish but also became more merciless than ever.

"Mohit, should we make her drunk?" Abhishek asked in a stammering tone.

"Yes! Of course."

"No! Otherwise she will not remember what we are going to do with her. We are here to enjoy and not to make her enjoy." These were the words of Rajesh.

This side everyone was happy at this suggestion of Rajesh whereas Niharika was trembling with fear that what they are going to do with her.

"Now we should start as it's' already 10O'clock." Mohit ordered them being their leader.

"Get naked as soon as possible." Prakash commanded her.

At the time she was undressing these five drunk rogues were sometime squeezing either her breasts, nipples, lips or her hips and she was moaning in pain.

"Now bend downwards." Now as Niharika had totally surrendered to her fate she was hardly caring who was giving the command and she was obediently following their instructions. As she bends downwards she felt a severe pain in her hips as someone had slapped hard from behind.

"Now get up!" Once again she was slapped and this process almost continued for thirty times.

"Now do a parade for us you slut!" As she started to parade in that room in front of those rapscallions; someone was abusing her, some were saying to stay straight and others were saying to sit down and as there were numerous command at a single time she got the slap most of the time whether she deserved or not.

"Now undress us!" And when she undressed these drunkards they commanded her to sit on her knees and all of them fucked her mouth as Prakash had done earlier. And the most pathetic situation was that they fucked her till the time they got ejaculated and most of the time the whole liquid was unable to spit and she had to engulf that nasty liquid.

"Now go on bed and open your legs as now you will get the orgasm." And as she followed her command all the five demons came together and started to torture her. One of them was fucking her mouth with his hands, two were engulfing her breasts and the other one was sucking her stomach and navel and their leader started fingering her vagina. And after few minutes when she started to moan he increased the intensity and finally she got the orgasm as these psychos had desired. But they were not contented. They made her two more orgasms changing the individuals.

She had almost broke now. She had no energy left. She was asking for pity with tears in her eyes but instead of pity she got nasty abuses and hard slaps. She was not finding any means of escape from this vex.

"She is thinking we are being cruel to her. I think we must make her see that how much lenient we are?"

And then they tied her legs and hands to the posts of the bed and shut her mouth by putting cloth in her mouth. And they started to whip her one by one with their belts on her each and every sensitive parts without caring what she was going through as this time she was not even independent for crying and she was moaning in unrecognised voice. And when almost they had made her fainted they untied her and gave her a bottle of water. This was the only thing which had brought her back to life otherwise she was almost sure that she would die of their beating. But the ordeal was not going to end. Then they decided to fuck her once again. But it was now literally impossible to face their torture and she almost shivered listening their decision. But she was totally helpless. And when Mohit started to fuck her, with each and every stroke she felt that she would die. Her body was now leaving its support and she was feeling unconsciousness. The last thing which she remembered before getting totally unconscious was that Prakash was tormenting her soul.

What was the fault of that girl who was totally devoted to her love and had started to dream on a different horizon? The only irony of this love is that you can yourself get fully committed but you can't assure other's commitment. This side Niharika was committed and that side Mohit was happy as for the first time after escaping from the cobwebs of arrogance he had got the privilege of making one of the eligible girl as his girlfriend which he hardly deserved. But this is the way how the teenage love goes in most of the cases. Why does God not create any mechanism that one could find that does the other person is worthy of his love or not? But perhaps this is life where the best and the worst happen on a consecutive basis and later on a majority basis. Here she was planning to spread this piece of lovely news to her old friends and there Mohit was busy in telling to his friends that how he grabbed the opportunity of getting a nice chick in his pond of swans whom he is going to make her serve as a sex slave on his birthday not only for him but also for them.

Oh! What an irony! For the same rectitude one person uses the best of the adjectives to describe his or her soulmate and the other one use the worst of the adjectives to describe her so called girlfriend which he rarely admits. He does not give her even the right to be called as her girlfriend as he considers her a slave, slut, whore, commodity of exotic pleasure, chick, babe and a hell lot of things which is enough to deteriorate the auspiciousness of this probity. But why does the God who is said to be very kind can't just give us an omen that the person for whom we are ready to put our life on stake is not even worthy of our unjust behaviour.

Oh! What an object this love is? A girl who labelled herself as the 'Silent Beauty' transformed into a 'Silent Sex Slave'. What an object this love is?

Chapter-18

❀ ❀ ❀

Oh! How much injustice was made by God to that friend heart? 'The God'; who is always advocated as the pater noster who takes the care of each and every injustice made to His child became so much insensitive that He didn't bother to have even a slight degree of pity towards His child. The girl who was immersed in the love of a boy whom she considered her life was such a demon she hadn't even dreamt of even in her dreams. How could God be so much harsh that He always punishes those people who are in true love and the crooks and the fillius nullius are left scot-free? Why does these great philosophers and theologists advocate the presence of God and His kind nature is still a million-dollar question? Perhaps this would be the reason that God has been described as an idea which people had created to fulfil their own illegitimate ambitions in His name. How can a person have belief on God when He is silently being the spectator when the soul and body of a girl is brutally tormented and no one comes even to console her at this juncture of time. Can God Himself tell us that what was the fault of that girl who had submitted her body and soul whom she loved and in return she got the most inhumane torture? Why people advocate about God that He is very merciful and kind? About which God they are advocating; who is just an idol or that God which really exists? But if God really exists then where He is? Where is He? Is He only present for being worshipped by us or taking the offerings from us in the form of cash and valuables? Then some of the so called scholars will say that had the God told you to worship Him or give him offerings in the form of cash and valuables? Then the million-dollar question is that if He has not told us to do these things then who had said that God is omnipresent. Bring that person and ask him about which Omnipresent he is talking about who was letting those lunatics torment her body one by one even when she was in unconscious state. And those outrageous demons left them on the gates of a hospital in her unconscious state in the weird state. If God is an epitome of justice; why didn't He cause their car into an accident so that they could get their desired punishment? But no! The God will punish those persons who are true and honest towards their life. He will give each and every privilege to those persons who deserve the severe punishment. Oh! What an inhumane scene it was to see her lying on the gates of a popular govt. hospital for hours where everything was popular except the way of treatment of the patients. How much a culprit is fearless even after giving a destination to his nasty activities that Abhishek called Jasmine in the morning and said her to receive her friend from the hospital? And before Jasmine could understand anything he disconnected the call without giving any further information. Jasmine got almost terror-stricken as she was unable to figure out how she could reach to the hospital when she had gone to his house and even if something had happened to her then why Abhishek is talking like this? But alas! How could poor Jasmine imagine that her sweet friend was no longer sweet as she was lying in an unconscious state from almost three hours? She hired an auto from the college to that hospital and she was almost literally fainted seeing the condition of her friend. Jasmine almost got hysterical after seeing the plight of her friend and she was unable to understand that how could this happen? In a matter of second she understood that what torment and torture her friend would have to endure and what these barbarians had done to her. She quickly lifted her and hired a cab and took her to one of the prestigious private hospital of the city as she knew that leaving her in this hospital would be like pushing her in a hell. And after completing the formalities she made Niharika admitted to one of the emergency ward. But the biggest problem was yet in front of her. How would she inform her parents? What would she say to them? But they had to be informed. She dialled the number of her father and told her to come as soon as possible as she had met an accident. What else she could say to them? Should she say them that your daughter is raped and she is lying in a hospital in coma? No! No! She haven't the enough courage to tell this nasty news to them directly. What would be the condition of their parents when they will hear that their Niharika had met with an accident, it was beyond Jasmine's imagination. And if she would have said that her sweet daughter had been raped or better say gang raped they would have died at once out of heart attack and horror. But Jasmine was wise enough to understand the gravity of the situation and dialled them once again and said them not to panic as she had admitted her to the hospital.

But these condolence were proving futile as how can the parent of a girl who had met an accident can remain calm and they headed towards the hospital on an emergency note.

Chapter-19

❀ ❀ ❀

There is no need to explain what would have been the state of the parents of Niharika when they get the first glance of their daughter lying on the bed in an emergency ward in coma struggling between life and death. After seeing the tormented condition of Niharika, her mother almost got literally fainted as she could not bear the grief which she had gone through in just a fraction of seconds. And when Jasmine sprinkled some water on her face, she got almost frantic as she hadn't imagined such an atmosphere for her daughter. Her father was almost in a panic state but anyhow he was holding his tears as it could make the situation graver. Jasmine was unable to assess the piece of information which can be imparted to her parents? She couldn't even gather enough courage to say them to stay calm at this juncture of time when lamenting was quite obvious. How could she say them not to lament and keep calm when their dear daughter was trapped into such an unfateful situation? Jasmine was herself feeling helpless as she was unable to annihilate their sufferings. If Nihu would have really met an accident, she would have said them to behave properly. As it is a quite obvious that a hospital is like a pilgrimage for the person who unwillingly confront to accident and Niharika was in the same situation in her parents' eyes. It had not been the case that their daughter was the only one who has gone through this stage but a lot of them are admitted here daily on a regular basis. But here the case was totally different. Her friend had been into such a situation where she can't even say her parents not to lament. And it was right that they were lamenting hoping that their Nihu had met an accident. Jasmine was terror-stricken at the fact what would happen when they come to know the reality. How would they respond when they would hear the hardcore truth?

"Jasmine, I want to meet the doctor." Niharika's father expressed his desire of meeting the doctor as it was of utmost importance at this point of time.

This was the toughest time for Jasmine as she was not able to figure out how could she take them to the doctor's cabin where their whole misconceptions which they had been raising from that time is going to end. And it was the fault of her oneself that she had told them a lie. But what could she have said about this boisterous havoc? It was perhaps the best way of delivering this news to them. She said the attendant to take care of Nihu's mother and she headed towards the cabin.

Dr. R.S Pathak, who was the in-charge of Niharika's case was a man of compassionate and kind nature was mature enough to understand the gravity of the situation.

He tried to ease the situation by offering both of them a comfortable chair and a glass of water. But can a glass of water and a comfortable chair in an A.C room heal the wounds of a father whose daughter is lying on the deathbed.

"Sir, what happened to my daughter? Sir, please tell me. What happened to her?" He was almost repeating the same question out of sheer tension.

"Mr. Ahuja! Even I am wondering how I could deliver you the news of your daughter; I am not understanding?" He would have said that there is nothing to worry and everything will be fine and that is expected from a doctor who is soaked in professionalism. But the doctor being a considerate guy having respect for human values tried to handle the situation by making aware of the real situation as telling them a lie would be only worsening the situation.

Mr. Ahuja was terror-stricken sensing any impending disaster.

"Sir, what happened to my dear Nihu? What happened to my baby?"

Mr. Pathak was not getting any clue that how could he transfer the news of this awful tragedy to him and he decided to be straightforward.

"Mr. Ahuja! I am extremely sorry to say that your daughter had been gang raped."

Niharika's father felt that someone had hit him with an iron rod on his face. And for the first time even being a man he started crying like a child. What was the fault of my baby that these mother-fuckers had tormented her soul? How could they do this to her? How can they be so inhumane that they didn't care for even a single second what they are doing? I will not leave that crooks. I will tear them apart. I will kill them. I will kill these droles. Then suddenly the voice of the doctor compelled him to confront the present.

"Mr. Ahuja! I am really feeling myself a culprit. But being a doctor, I can't hide the facts as hiding the facts would only worsen the situation. The problem is more severe as we had expected. She has not been only raped by multiple fillius nullius a number of times but also she had been terribly abused. They had brutally whipped all over her body and the sensitive parts of her body had been whipped severely. I am feeling fearful to say that it would take a long time to bring her back in a well condition. Her body parts have been so much tortured that I can't explain you in normal terminology. You would think being a father that I am exaggerating the facts but if I try to be honest I am shivering while telling you that even though we try hard we can't bring her in a normal condition. I can't arrogate to give you any false hopes which may prove a nine days wonder for you. After few months of treatment her body could be in a well condition but she had got a high degree of mental setback. God forbid me to say these words but I am fearing that you could never get your baby in a normal condition! When she would be discharged from here she would have been transformed into an insane girl who had to be admitted in a mental asylum."

Mr. Pathak spoke all the sentence in a row as he did not want to give this news into bits and parts.

And this side, Mr. Ahuja was feeling that with each and every word someone was slicing his heart into infinite number of pieces. Even the tears of his eyes went dry and his mind got blank. It seemed that he became motionless. As Jasmine was aware what was going to happen in the doctor's cabin, even being a girl she was trying to console Mr. Ahuja as this was only thing she could do at this juncture of sorrow and agony. But as it has been said that the tyranny of evil do not set its prey easily and Jasmine was wise enough to understand what was going to happen when Mrs. Ahuja listens the tale of this catastrophe. She decided to narrate this catastrophe herself to Mrs. Ahuja as Mr. Ahuja was not in a situation to speak anything as he had got almost such a setback that he had become literally speechless. She took her to the emergency ward and when Mrs. Ahuja asked what had happened seeing the plight of her husband; Jasmine consoled her that nothing weird had happened and took her away from there. Finally when Jasmine felt that at least Mrs. Ahuja is in a slight comfortable condition which she knew is irrelevant narrated her whole saga. What a miserable and devastating scene it was that even the angels of heaven would have been weeping seeing the condition of Mrs. Ahuja. She was screaming in the loudest voice which her body can support and it seems that there was no end of her lamenting. She was getting continuously unconscious and whenever Jasmine made her conscious by sprinkling water she started to scream and blame her daughter's bad luck and her own bad luck.

Oh! What an object this love is even? Why people are so lenient towards love till now it is a matter of debate? Which love they always advocate? Why they consider it a virtue? Why they say it a blessing of God? Why? Why? Why they consider it generous which can change a person life. Yes, of course it is generous. It is so much compassionate that it had put a cheerful and bubbly girl into coma from where she would not recover for her whole life and will spend the whole life in a mental asylum. Yes, it is so much altruistic in nature that two persons had been totally broke and they are in such a good condition that one has become woeful; unable to utter a single word to describe the plight to his own wife and the other one is so happy that she is screaming out loud in sheer agony that she is getting unconscious repeatedly. It is such a pious rectitude that a girl who should spend her time either in a college or on a holiday trip is spending her time in an emergency ward beside her friend who is in coma and trying to console her parents. Why people falsely advocate this odious crap as the most beautiful part of life? It is understandable that a common man is like a flock of sheep but what would they say about our great philosophers and scholars who always advocate in favour of this so called love. Why don't they come and see what this innocent girl and her parents are going through in such a deplorable state? Are they blind or deaf and dumb towards these catastrophe? It is a common phenomenon to always blame the girls and women for betraying their partner and they also advertise this betrayal with pomp and show with their so called sad songs, ghazals, shayaris and a hell lot of things. But the million dollar question is that had they ever find a single case where she had camouflaged his partner by doing gang rape with her friends and tormenting him as a sex slave for a whole night tormenting his body, heart and soul for whole night to such an extent that he would be unconscious and even if he recovered he would spend his whole life in a mental asylum. The only answer be a big **No.** But our so called scholars will again advocate that there are a lot of people in mental asylum and that only because they have been deceited by a girl. But if they make their eyes open in a genuine way they would find that similar number of girls are in a mental asylum who are there just because of the Judas kiss of these nefarious idiots.

Then why do they advocate this crap as a blessing which only bring sorrow for each and every person directly or indirectly attached to this holy shit.

"Jasmine, the patient had opened her eyes. You can meet her." A nurse came to spread this good piece of news which was most needed at this point of time.

And as Mrs. Ahuja got the requisite lifeline for her survival; she wiped her tears and went from there to see their daughter's rebirth.

Chapter-20

❊ ❊ ❊

When Jasmine entered the ward with Mrs. Ahuja she was unable to determine should she be happy to see her friend once again in a conscious state or should she feel sorry for her parents? How could she face Mr. Ahuja who was almost keening at her daughter's condition even though she had got conscious after so many hours? And not only his father but also her mother started to lament as soon as she glanced at her daughter. Jasmine was in a totally perplexed condition as she didn't have any idea how to respond. On one side she was happy after finding her friend in a conscious state and on the other side she was totally in despair seeing her parent's condition. Both of them were mewling and only mewling continuously and not uttering a single word. Were these the tears of happiness which were sprouting after finding their daughter alive or were it the tears of a parent who was forced to see their daughter in such a deteriorated condition? What was this? Jasmine was not finding courage this time to meddle at this juncture where each and every tears was carrying a different meaning.

But perhaps the toughest phase which a person is bound to endure was being endured by Niharika. She didn't have enough energy in her body so that she can cry at least in front of her parents and her friend. She was continuously sobbing and her each and every sob was narrating a different tale. Oh! How much pitiful is that when everyone is praying for your well-being, you pray to God for your mortality. She was wondering why God had made her alive. How would she face the eyes of her parents who were continuously lamenting and blood were coming in their tears. What would she tell to her parents that their unfortunate daughter is so much unfateful that now she doesn't want to live? What would she say to her mother that the daughter whom you had adored more than your life has been in this hell as she had made a blunder by finding a false intimacy to a rascal in the outside world of this odious society? What would she say to her father that her princess whom he used to believe more than her mother breached his belief as she had started to believe that there is something called love which is not less than a shit? What would she tell her friend Jasmine who had been in the hospital taking her care like a mother that she got into this hell as she thought that she is worthy of the holy shit which will make her life worse than the shit itself? Why God Why?

"Why had he done this to me? What was my fault...? Why had he done this to me? What was my fault? Why had he...?" These were the first words which Jasmine and her parents heard since they had come to the hospital.

"Nothing will happen my dear. We are with you. We have now came na baby! We will not…." They tried to console her baby but before Mr. and Mrs. Ahuja could complete their lines, their princess once again got unconscious. And both of them again started lamenting.

"Uncle, please don't snivel in front of her as she is already feeling culprit in her own eyes and you are making her feel worse." Jasmine suggested as she could understand what her friend would have been going through.

Even though they were trying hard not to cry but how can they stop themselves from crying. But keeping in mind the suggestion of Jasmine they tried not to show their emotions in front of their daughter. But if this would have been the remedy they would have done this also but even Jasmine suggestions were proving futile as Niharika was getting conscious for some time and getting unconscious repeatedly. It seemed that she had got unhinged as every time she got conscious she started to sob and repeating only two sentences continuously and these cursed sentences were 'Why had he done this to me? What was my fault?'

Chapter-21

❖ ❖ ❖

It was the tyranny of the fate that had made Mr. and Mrs. Ahuja to reach in the emergency ward of Apollo Hospital of Pune from the streets of Gaya. A town where people from all over the world come to perform rituals which could give the so called peace to their ancestors' soul. And it was the fate of this couple that they were praying to God for enlightment of their daughter's soul which had been tormented by those obstinates. After a month when Niharika was discharged from the hospital and was brought to her own house; her parents were still in agony seeing the plight of her princess. How their lovely princess who used to wave a magical atmosphere in the house was just repeating that two cursed lines unaware of her state of mind? How would they send the part of their soul to a mental asylum? How would they send that bubbly girl who was a source of inspiration and pride of their house? How much ungrateful they were that they can't even tell their two other child what had happened to their elder sister that had made her totally broke. Even though it had been a month but still they were not ready to believe that their part of soul had been deteriorated to such an extent and they are so much helpless that they are not able to do anything for her well-being. All the so called **Mannats, Pujas** and everything which they had done for years would become so much unrealistic as these things are of no use in the practical world. Who says that a man gets the result of his own doings? Then can for God sake can anyone would tell them that what sin both of the husband and wife had committed that their child got such a harsh punishment from this merciless God. How would they send their princess to that place where no one wants to go even in his wildest dream? Even the hell is a better destination than a mental asylum.

But they were not only helpless but also the victim of this bloody time-frame. They had to face the reality. They were optionless. They had to take this hardcore decision for the well-being of their daughter's life. And with heavy heart both husband and wife headed for Ranchi to put their princess into a place which was far worse than a hell.

What a heart-breaking scene it was to see both of them crying like a child when the attendant of asylum was taking her to the specified ward and they just like a spectator were forced to see their soul going away from them.

What a sombre object these worldly affairs are? On one side they wanted to die as now they don't have enough courage to face further torment but they had to live for their two other children. And with heavy heart and tears in their eyes they returned their home which was once again lonely without their beloved child.

PART-2

AFTER EIGHTEEN MONTHS

Chapter-22

❊ ❊ ❊

03rd January; Thursday; 07:30 AM

Unaware of the whole world and its' worldly affairs Niharika was bound to spend her life in the mental asylum where she was admitted almost eighteen months before. Even her parents had left the hope of getting her back in a normal state. But as it has been said that the best thing about bad time is that it passes someday and perhaps that someday had came when Niharika found a girl in the same weird condition as she was. In the playground of the asylum when she finds a girl uttering almost the same lines which she had been repeating from the last eighteen months, she feels that there is some connection of these lines. Seeing the plight of the girl she starts to recall something which had been almost buried in the deep corner of her brain. Her revival or better say the recalling of her past was not as easy as we are used to see in a movie or a television soap. As it has been said that when we try to recall our past, we get tears and sufferings. Then what would have Niharika endured in recalling her past needs no explanation? Each and every moment which had dragged her to this hell was revolving around her eyes. She was feeling how she could be so ungrateful that she had been here from the last eighteen months. But her one thought reminded her that even though now she had recovered practically she should consider this asylum as her home pretending that she has not recovered. Her this thought was the by-product of our own rotten society which sees a rape victim as the real culprit instead of those swindlers. But her one thought demanded to be released as she had already given a lot of pain and suffering to her parents and now she can't give them more sufferings. If even now when she had recovered and pretends what she will say to her own soul that she had become so mean that she barely cares those persons who are her parents who had laid their eyes from months in the hope of seeing their daughter in a normal condition.

No! No! I will return to my home where my family is waiting for me. I don't bother about this society. It doesn't matter for me what they back-bite or condemn me, I will return for my family. I am not like other girls whose life comes to an end when they are raped. That odious stolids should feel shame and remorse; not me. I will start a new life from here. I will show those astute that I am not finished and I can live that life once again which I was enjoying. I will go. I will go.

***

If the life would have been so simple, life couldn't have been called life. Niharika made up her mind to go back her home. After clearing all the formalities she goes to the senior doctor who is responsible for granting permanent leave to get his final signature and wishing him heartiest congratulations as only due to his caring attitude it had been possible.

"Hey sir, I am really happy as just because of your efforts, I became fine. I am really thankful to you. Thank you sir. Please sign the final medical report and I will get permanent leave from here."

"Ok! Can I see your reports?"

"Of course sir." She handed him the reports.

And when the doctor sees her medical report and makes such a frowned face that once again let her to tremble as now she didn't wanted to be the prey of any mishappenings.

"I am signing your application and report…"

"Oh! So much of thank you sir! Thank you sir." The excitement was crystal clear on her face.

"Let me complete my words. I am signing your application and report as its' my duty and my obligation. I had read your reports. You had been gang raped and I am wondering what you will do after going back? For the first time in my life I have seen such a shameless girl who wants to go back to mainstream of the society. Had you ever thought what would you do? You will once again trap a rich guy in front of your beauty and will take money in exchange of your body. At least those girls who trap and take money from rich guys are far better than bitches like you. Prostitutes like you who are used to have multiple sex partners will once again invite yourself a bunch of guys to satiate your hunger of sex. And when they will not give you money as you had invited them yourself you would make a false case of gang rape. I can't understand how much hunger you have for sex. Even the prostitutes and call-girls prefer sex with a single person at a time. But I think that you are the biggest whore of the world who needs five guys at a single time. How much money you had demanded from those guys that they felt unable to fulfil? Whores like you are blot on the society. Don't you have even such a slight degree of shame that how would you confront your parents? Oh! Sorry, I forgot that these are those sagacious blots who give birth to a girl so that they can sell her body and can earn money for enjoying a sybaritic life. Can you tell me one thing; is your mother also a prostitute? How much she takes? More or less than you?

Even now if you feel that you have little shame left; go from here but don't show your face to the society. Society consists of civilized persons like us and not whores like you. Whore like you are a just a blot on the society."

Niharika was standing there silently listening his each and every words being emotionless. The moment she had decided to go back she had made up her mind to bear those craps and satires which people deliver to the victim as they feel privileged for passing such shits. And she took the letter from the doctor and headed towards the gate where she would never desire to come again.

Finally when she came out of the gate she felt contented to see her parents as they had come to take their baby to home. She was thanking her stars that when everyone is neglecting her, at least her parents had came to take her not bearing any misconceptions in their mind.

"Look Nihu! Who has came with us to take you to your home?" Mr. Ahuja pointed to the other direction.

What a pleasant surprise it was for Niharika that her best friend Jasmine had came to take her. Oh! How much she was feeling obliged to see Jasmine at the place where she needed her the most. But it was not less than the best gift of the life of Jasmine when Mrs. Ahuja informed that Niharika has now recovered. She couldn't stop herself from coming even from Pune to her Nihu's house as she wanted to meet her friend who has now recovered from her horrible past. And all of them headed towards Mr. Ahuja's house with happiness and calmness on everyone's face.

Chapter-23

❄ ❄ ❄

After coming home, Niharika's parents arranged a private party in which the only family members were included including Jasmine who was not less than a family member for them. After the party got over Jasmine had to go back to college as her flight was in the evening. Even after repeated resistance from Niharika she didn't stay as she didn't want to ruin the private moment of Ahuja family which was most needed at this point of time. The Niharika's parents were thinking how to console their child as the forthcoming disaster in tits and bits was yet to come in the form of comments and satires. They decided to make understand their child the hardcore reality of this stern society so that she cannot feel culprit in her own eyes for the rest of her life.

"Niharika, can we have a talk with you, if you are feeling comfortable and if you don't mind."

"Yes, of course dad." Niharika was dying to have a private conversation with her parents.

"Look Nihu! Now when you have recovered by the grace of Almighty you should feel thankful to God." Her mother initiated the string of the conversation.

"Hmmm...."

"Nihu! We know that a lot of things would be running in your mind. Your past would have been hovering in your mind. Even though you try hard, the memories of your past will be haunting your mind from time to time. But it would be my sincere suggestion that please for god sake don't ever let them ruin your values. The time will come when you will let yourself responsible for this ordeal but never let yourself down. Remember one thing that those obnoxious rascals were the culprits and not you. Never feel that you had been the reason of anyone's misery. Sometime whenever you would see us sad you would feel that we are sad due to you but this would be one of the few misconceptions which would let you down. You are our princess as always and will remain forever...." Her mother was trying her best to prepare her child mentally to face the society.

"It might happen" her father continued the conversation "that you would sometimes feel that whole world had been framing a conspiracy against you and you would blame your luck and curse the god for the whole saga. But this would be one of the few elements which will prompt to let your morale down. The time would come a lot of times when you will lose your confidence. But Nihu! Never lose your confidence as the person who had lost his confidence has lost everything in his life. You would feel sometimes that your whole world has came to a standstill and there are no ways to escape but you would have always to remember that tough times never last, tough people do. It will be your sheer determination which will make you stand in this society. This society always prompts a person to have inferiority towards oneself. But you know na Nihu, the person who has got the disease of inferiority complex can never stand. You are quite yourself an intelligent girl and you know how to tackle with these problems. The time will come..."

"When you would feel" her mother interrupted "that why I, why it has happened only to me? But remember my child; there are few things in life which are beyond our control. Only you should know how to tackle the inevitable and non-inevitable phases of life. Not being a mother, but being a woman I am saying you this thing that you would feel hatred towards this man community as you would label each and every man as a crook and lusty and this would be your biggest mistake and this would be the point where you will miss your mark. Remember that there have been men who had put their life on stake for their charmante and there are girl who have sacrificed their each and everything for the men. There would be times when this ferocious society will try to let you down at every moment by their nasty piece of satires which will almost make you feel that you have been torn apart and the life will seem as a burden which can't be bore anymore. But this would be the test of your mental toughness and strength as your dad said that tough times never last but tough people do. Nihu! It would be only your sheer determination and your unending will of getting high in your life which will keep your life in motion. Always remember that we are the one who let ourselves down and we are the same person who keeps our mind and heart in a high esteem. My baby once again I am repeating never let your pride and confidence down so that anyone could get the chance to let you down. If anyone makes you down, he should not be blamed as you would be solely responsible for inviting them to intrude in your life. And one should especially never let anyone make him down and destroy her ethics and values when one is going through the toughest phase of her life. You were Niharika Ahuja and you will always be Niharika Ahuja only and only if you are willing to remain Niharika Ahuja."

Oh! What a pious scene it was when both Mr. and Mrs. Ahuja were trying to restore back their child's confidence which was of the utmost importance at this juncture of time. After that they wished her good luck for her new life and blessed her with their blessings which were going to be a life-changer in her new inning of life all of them went to their own bedroom with a rediscovered state of mind.

Chapter-24

❖ ❖ ❖

08thJanuary; 05:30 AM; Tuesday

What a sin had Niharika committed in the name of love, even she was unable to assess. Whether her life was cursed by any evil spirits or was there any witch of her past birth that was not leaving its hold on Niharika that her fate was each and everytime giving her such a setback which were deadlier than the previous one. What would she say to herself when each and everytime she got a new setback. People always argue about the existence of God and his unseen blessings in our life. But had anyone even peeped into the life of Niharika, he would have lose faith in the existence of God? What was the fault of that cheerful girl that she was regularly stabbed by the fate and her heart and soul were torn apart to such an extent that even the humanity would have been shedding blood-tears. When Niharika woke up in the morning with cries of her siblings, she was unable to understand that what had happened to these guys. But the scene which she had seen was almost unbearable for any tough guy. Who says that the motivational quotes are not only bookish language which only falsely advertises that they can change any human's life from misery to a better note? What would she say to those tenacious idiots who falsely give us a wrong hope of making our life better? She had not even spent a single day of her new inning and God had given such a setback that can't be endured. She was almost torn apart when she found that her parents had committed suicide the last evening after making her understand and taking promise from her that at any damn cost she will never even think of taking her own life. Who says that the worldly affairs are an important ingredient of a person's well-being? Which worldly affair they were talking about? A world which had been especially designed to rob each and every happiness from her life. Was it less painful that she had been deceived as no one had been ever deceived that the God had snatched her parents? It was almost impossible for her to keep control on herself. And when she found a piece of paper which was the so called suicide note was more than enough to make her believe that this world is just a lethal ground for the people who believe in humanity and morality.

What a heart-touching letter it was!

Dear Nihu!

We would ask for forgiveness from our dear Nihu a million times as we are taking this tough decision without giving you any clue in advance. It is also the toughest decision of our life as we are leaving you alone in this shallow world. We are your culprit as we are leaving you at the moment when you need us the most. We know that we are being selfish but we had no choice left. We know that you would be wondering what is the difference between those astutes and us who had left you torn apart. How can we make you understand that we were being so much helpless that we had been helpless? We are not trying to justify our vice but the fact that is we couldn't hold it anymore. We tried our best to keep ourselves alive but how can a person remain alive when he has been torn apart to such an extent that he had no willingness to live further? How can we see our daughter for whole life in tears and blaming herself for the mistake which she hadn't committed? Even though we tried hard to keep ourselves alive but what could we do to escape from this stern society. The society which regularly stab you every moment with her satires which are unable to bear. We would have bore all those nasty words but how can we bear that someone uses those nasty words for our princess. How can we make understand ourselves that these are the words which will not only create havoc for our life but also for my child and we are so much helpless that we can't do anything? We can bear every troughs of life but we can't bear any trough which could create problem for you. We know that when you would be finding difficult to make yourself subtle we are endowing you with responsibility of standing alone in this vicious society. But we know our child is so much brave and so much wise that she will understand our helplessness and will create a new meaning out of her life. We were torn apart from inside but it was our heartiest wish to see our princess for one more time in a normal condition. Finally when this dream came true we had no any other dream to fulfil and perhaps this is the appropriate time to leave this mortal world.

Once again we are asking forgiveness for committing this sin and leaving you alone. But our blessings will be with you always and our soul will be directing you in any case of trough of life. Once again we are sorry our child. And always remember you were our brave Niharika Ahuja and you will always remain our brave Niharika Ahuja.

Yours And Always Yours
Your Cursed Mom & Dad

***

What could a person expect from a girl who has came to the so called normal state after spending almost eighteen months in a mental asylum and she loses her both parents in just a matter of twenty-four hours? Even it is tough to imagine that what would have been the mental state of that girl. Leave that girl for a second; even the toughest mind would get almost hysterical after such a disastrous incident. And when we think about Niharika, even thinking about her mental state makes us shiver. For the first time she was not in a state that she can cry even as this privilege has also been snatched from this so called God as

He had made her so much cry in the past that almost her tears had drained up. She was not in a position to think even as her whole mind had gone blank. And this was the time when she was not blaming anyone for this catastrophe as she had made her mind almost that it was in her destiny that is not going to change forever. Even if she would blame, whom she would blame? Should she blame that escrocs, herself, the God or this rotten society? Even if she would blame anyone what's the use of blaming anyone, because blaming is not going to change her destiny. The destiny which that God had written is not going to change even though she tries hard. And that's why she was not thinking anything else. She had become thoughtless, motionless, and emotionless and God knows what more.

But how could a person get rid of the worldly affairs? Even though she was not getting enough courage to make her heart calm but she had to perform the rituals of the funeral processions. With blank mind and heavy heart she completed the funeral processions as it is a common phenomenon that we try to get over with the funeral processions as soon as possible if any person commits suicide. As she returned to her house after the rituals she was astonished to see Jasmine once again.

"Why have you came Jasmine? That's my fate and how long will you support me?"

"As long as I am alive. I am your friend Nihu! Why are you saying like this? Your brother told me about this tragic incident and I had came by return flight as soon as I heard about this tragedy.

"I don't want to snatch your happiness and ruin your life. I have made my life a hell and I don't want that you are pulled in this avernus."

Jasmine didn't replied anything but she was mature enough to understand the psyche of Niharika at this moment. What have been running inside Niharika's head didn't need any explanation and Jasmine could understand these things. She decided to stay with Niharika for few days as it was the best she could do from her side. As she started to stay with her, she found drastic change in her behaviour. She couldn't understand that she started to remain silent for hours without being aware of her environment. Jasmine could understand her silence which was a common phenomenon after such tragedies but her unusual silence started to bother her. She was fearful regarding Nihu's mental state as just a few days had passed that her friend had came from the mental asylum and she didn't want to see her friend in that hell once again. She was unable to decide what she could do for her friend as leaving her in this situation could end her life. After a lot of thinking she decided to contact her uncle Bernard Oscar Backefield as he was one of the famous psychiatrist in Indore. Jasmine was shocked to hear after explaining the case and symptoms that it was case of depression as her mind had been attacked with multiple setback due to this sudden tragic incident. And she took her friend to

Indore so that she could bring her back in her normal state.

"Uncle, she always remains silent and her silence makes me fearful."

"Jasmine, don't take tension. Everything will be fine. We will try to cure her problem and the exact situation could be clear only when we would diagnose her disease after the initial check-ups."

"Hmmm…"

And when they went to the hospital the next day; Jasmine was praying to God for her well-being when her friend was in the lab for the check-ups. And when they got the medical report; Jasmine went to her uncle's clinic. She was in more tension as this was the toughest time as he was going to tell her that what had exactly happened.

"Jasmine, there is nothing to worry. She had some mild setbacks which had turned into depression. It can be cured easily." Mr. Backefield passed his statements after having a careful look towards her report.

"Thanks uncle. How much time it will take?" She felt a sense of relaxation on her face and she was eager to take back her friend as soon as possible."

"Being honest, it will take almost five to six months. But you have no need to worry. She is safe and fine here. I am allocating her a special ward where her utmost care would be taken and she will not face any problem. She is just like a daughter to me. Jasmine, I am proud of you that you had gone to such an extent for your friend. God bless you my child. I advise you to return back to your college and focus on your studies and come here occasionally. And don't take any tension regarding your friend. She will be fine on a permanent basis."

"Thanks uncle. What would be the medical fees incurred in the whole treatment?"

"We could talk about that later also. Firstly you focus on your studies and let me concentrate on her treatment."

"Thanks uncle. Thanks a lot."

After admitting her friend in her uncle's clinic she headed for the college the very next day.

Chapter-25

❀ ❀ ❀

12th June; Tuesday

Finally after six months when Niharika came out of the clinic, the person who was happier than Niharika itself was Jasmine. It was the generosity of Mr. Backefield that he cared about Niharika more than he would have taken the care of her own daughter. Mr. Backefield generosity didn't end to just caring of her patient but it was also crystal clear in the medical bill. He had charged the minimum for her treatment. And when Jasmine was walking out of the clinic she could see a different Niharika. Was it the magic of the sessions of her uncle or Niharika had found a different meaning of life; she was not able to understand but she was happy. She was happy as she got back her friend for the second time. She was happy as her own parents were happy seeing the concern for her friend. She was happy because she herself had also found a different meaning of the life where the unpredictability is the most unpredictable object. And from there she went to Niharika's house so that she could take at least a glance over her brother and sister who were left on the mercy of God. Niharika was happy to find that her brother and sister are residing in her maternal uncle's house comfortably. But at the same time she felt miserable to find out that her uncle had taken care of her siblings but they didn't bothered even for a single time to see that is she alive or not? And it was just due to the fact that she was a rape victim and they didn't want to let their image down by giving her shelter. But soon these thoughts withered away as she had been used to such discriminations.

And as Jasmine could feel the changing pattern on Nihu's face she tried to handle the situation.

"Today you are giving me a party where you are going to cook my favourite dishes for me."

"Its' ok yar!"

Once again when after an hour they sat together for enjoying the dishes, the conversation soon turned to the previous incidents.

"Jasmine! I will not leave those scoundrels."

"I understand. I can understand your feelings."

"No Jasmine, I have no feelings left. I am serious. I will not leave those rogues." Her voice was becoming serious with each and every word.

"But Niharika, if you don't feel bad I would say that its' almost impossible. Why are you trying to ruin your life once again? Leave those swindlers and start a new life." Jasmine tried to handle the situation seeing the gravity of the situation.

"You know Jasmine; my life has already been ruined. And you know nothing is impossible. I can't be at peace till these rapacious rapists are alive." Her voice was getting grave.

"If you have decided to take revenge, then I am always with you. But we should also consider the practical problems which are going to come. It will need a great deal of planning and professionalism. And one thing more, it will need a lot of money." She made her aware of the hardcore realities which are going to come in this expedition.

"No Jasmine! You had already put a lot of pain for me. Now I don't want you to indulge in these things. You have a great life ahead. Enjoy your life. I don't know my future and I don't want to ruin your future." Niharika warned her and at the same time she didn't want to put her friend in danger just because of her.

"You know Niharika that I can't leave you. I am your friend and I don't want to listen these craps that you don't want to ruin my life and all sorts of these things. If you will keep me out of this expedition, I will blame myself for my whole life that in this life I was not so much worthed that I can earn a true friend." Her voice was commanding but full of sobs.

"Its' not like that Jasmine. You are the only whom I trust more than myself. If you will say like that I will not forgive myself for my whole life." Niharika felt that she shouldn't have said these words.

And when finally they agreed to be companions in this expedition of revenge, they hugged each other tightly and felt that they have got a new source of energy. Now it was the time to discuss the problems which they were going to encounter. And after brainstorming for almost three hours they made a list of the possible hassles.

"Look, Nihu! These are one of the few expected hassles leaving the unexpected. And these are:

1. *Money Problem:* For this mission we are going to need a lot of money which is currently beyond our capabilities if we take a glance at our bank accounts and belongings.

2. *Target Problem:* Each and every of the knaves are in different city as the college had been over and it would be really difficult to find them.

3. *Method of Killing:* As both of us are girls, it would be very hard to find weapons even from the black market and so we would have to think a lot upon how we are going to kill them.

4. *Travelling Problem:* It might also happen that we have to travel a lot across whole India and it can create a problem in the execution of our mission.

5. *Police and CBI Problem:* As we start to execute our plan, we will come in the eyes of police and CBI which can make our mission come to a halt instantly.

6. *Planning Problem:* It might happen that any particular plan can fail and we can put ourselves into great problem.

7. *Hiring Problem:* As we are only two in number it is impossible without a temporary team. And the problem will be created as we both are girls and how we will hire the appropriate people at appropriate times.

8. *Betrayal Problem:* As we would be hiring different people at different time purely on money basis and they would have neither any emotion nor motivation attached to the mission they can betray us easily if they get more money.

9. *Counter-Attack Problem:* We should also keep in mind that they can devise a counter plan for us and can counter-attack on us. And this would be the biggest hassle.

10. *Time Problem:* As we are very much enthusiastic regarding our mission it might happen that we would feel hasty and this would spoil our whole planning. We have to be very patient as the importance of timing will be the most crucial factor in the execution.

"That's great! And as far as my mind goes, there should be no more hassles." Excitement was crystal clear on both girls' faces.

As they had diagnosed all the possible hassles which they were going to come through they decided to work upon one problem at a single time. They decided to work upon the biggest problems of this mission and that was the 'Money Problem'. When they sat together once again after a coffee break, they started to calculate how much money they had in their possession? Niharika was feeling very tensed as she had only 75,000 Rs in her bank accounts and she had no jewelleries left. All the jewelleries had been sold for her treatment already. Jasmine had almost 2.5 lacs in her personal account and she had jewelleries of worth 1 lakh and surely even after adding both these sums were in any way not enough for the mission. Or if they would try to be honest it was not even enough for them to survive their mission for few days. Once again after a serious brainstorming they came on a conclusion that they will take the help of Mr. Backefield. They decided that Niharika will sell her few ancestral property to Mr. Backefield and she would give the reason that as that city had been a haunted place for her, she wants to leave the city.

The very next day when she called him to inform that she wants to sell her ancestral property, Mr. Backefield showed an interest in her ancestral property. For the first time favour was in her favour as even before explaining the reasons why she wants to sell her property he seemed enthusiastic and it made her way easy. As Mr. Backefield had got a chance to harvest the seeds of his generosity and he didn't want to ruin the chance of purchasing properties at a place which had been described an international heritage at his own cost. Seeing the urgency of Niharika he decided to give her whole sum as an advance but even Niharika knew that the price which he was offering was far less than the real price. But neither the property nor these things mattered for her as she was rejoicing at the solution of her biggest problem. And in a matter of 15 days she sold few of her ancestral property and got more than 75 lacs in her account.

Chapter-26

❋ ❋ ❋

Once again they got together in Niharika house to execute the further planning. They were very happy at the successful initiation of their mission. Now when they start to discuss the further course of action Niharika was worried as she couldn't get an idea how to locate these rascals. And as they had firstly decided to teach the real culprit; Mohit Chandra a lesson, they were not getting any clue to track him. But as it had been said that if there is a will, there is a way, they soon found a mind-blowing idea.

"Is it possible?" Niharika exclaimed at Jasmine's idea.

"Of course. He was one of the best student of the college in academics as we all know. And in the placements he would have got one of the best package and college would have surely displayed his name on website. And from there we can find that in which city this rogue is currently residing."

"Hmmm…"

And when they started to search their college website they were delighted to find that his name was there and he was placed in Jaipur in Wipro.

"But Jasmine, there is one major problem. Will your parents allow you to go with me to Jaipur and all other places?"

"Chill yar! I had sorted this problem in advance. The day when we had decided to sell your ancestral property to my uncle, I had told my parents that I got a job offer in Coimbatore so that they can't come to meet me frequently as it is far enough from my house. And as my uncle sensed that you are selling property for something else I said clearly to my uncle that I am going to stay with you and my parents shouldn't know. And for his this generosity he can get more property in such a less cost if needed. Do you think that you only know that he was taking undue advantage of our emergency, I was also well aware that this Mr. Backefield was making us fool. But for the execution of our plan, it is necessary to make some sacrifices."

"Jasmine, you are really genius. You have solved my biggest tension." There was a sense of calmness and peace on her face.

"Ok! Ok! Now make preparations for the journey. We will start for Jaipur day after tomorrow."

Chapter-27

❋ ❋ ❋

After reaching to the Jaipur station, they firstly decided to take room in a hotel till the time Jasmine would not find the exact location of his office and his flat. They booked a room in Vesta International which was just 2 km from the railway station for three days as they had put a deadline of three days for searching his address. It was the sheer efficiency of Jasmine that not only she located his residence and office but she also rented a flat in Sindhi Colony which was his residence. And at the end of three days they got themselves settled in a flat.

"But, Jasmine what is our plan? Now when we have come here, what will we do?" There was anxiety on Niharika's face.

"We will do nothing. We will just follow the principle of 'Wait and Watch' and will remain patient." Jasmine replied in a calm tone.

Both girls started to live together. Even before a week would have passed Jasmine took admission in an institute for the preparation of CAT. Niharika started to pass her idle time either watching movies or thinking about the further course of action.

***

"Excuse me Mam. If you don't mind and if I am right you are Jasmine Backefield and you used to study in Symbiosis University. Do you recognise me?" Mohit was exclaimed to find Jasmine at this place.

"Oh! Yes. Who can forget you? You were the most handsome and most intelligent guy of our college." Jasmine replied with a fake smile. But she actually wanted to say that how can I forget you mother-fucker? It was only you who had made my friend's life worse than a hell and you are going to pay for it.

"Its' not like that. What are you doing here?"

"You know everyone is not intelligent like you and that's why I didn't have any job. And now I am preparing for CAT so that at least I can get a good college for my MBA." She once again passed her fake smile.

"I think you have came quite recently and that's why I haven't seen you earlier."

"Yes, of course. I have came one month before. And if I am right, you live in this colony."

"Oh! How much stupid I am? We had been neighbours from last one month and we hadn't seen each other. But now we can meet each other as classmates or friends if you don't mind." He was baffled at his own stupidity.

"Its' ok. But how will I contact you? You are quite a busy person and I also get my classes off on Saturdays and

Sundays." She was wondering to tell him that tell me bastard how can I keep track of your movements?

"Oh! This is my card. You can ring me anytime between 7 P.M to 9 A.M. And anytime on saturday and sunday."

"Ok! Bye."

"Ok! Bye."

And when Jasmine came back to her flat, she told this news of encounter with that rapscallion to Niharika and suggested her to live in a hotel on Saturday and Sunday every week as it may happen that he can see her by chance and it will ruin the whole planning. And as decided Niharika started to leave for hotel on these two days and this side Jasmine started to cement her friendship with that nocent. The time flew and Jasmine made him believe that this friendship had transformed into love and the day also came when Mohit proposed her. She readily accepted her proposal and now they were couples. Sometimes Niharika would wonder had this rascal also spread his magic wand on Jasmine that she always talks to him. And as it had been said that girls' are doubtful in nature she used to have doubt on her friend that had she been really into love with that malefactor? What an object this love is that even though a person is totally torn apart he feels the momentary love for that person. But Jasmine was mature enough not to commit this blunder which had let his best friend's world came to an end. Jasmine behaviour towards Mohit was so much lenient that any person couldn't doubt that she was setting a trap and it was not any love. She was engrossed in Mohit so much that even Niharika started feeling envious of Jasmine indirectly. And Jasmine had already sensed but she was wise enough not to be distracted by few emotional barriers and lack of co-ordination from her own friend. She understood the fact that the fate had already done a lot of injustice to her Nihu and if Nihu was having such type of feelings towards her, she was right in her own place. She knew the very basic philosophy of girls' that they are sensitive and emotional in nature and any girl wouldn't bear the fact that her own friend would have even a false affair with a guy whom she used to love at one point of her life.

But Jasmine was keeping patience as she knew the value of timing in this mission. Finally the time came when she had her birthday on 13th Jan and she gave the invitation to come to her flat two days prior. And it was now the time that one day before the execution of her plan she would have to shed all the doubts and misconceptions of her friend. And when on 12th January she announced the high time for the execution of her plan and told her in detail the reason for waiting such a long time, Niharika was feeling ashamed to doubt on such a genuine personality. She was crying and labelling herself as nasty, unlucky and a hell lot of adjectives as she had done the blunder. Then in spite of saying anything to her, Jasmine explained her the **'Coordination Problem'** in detail which is quite common during such type of missions in which a partner starts to doubt on other partner and where the coordination starts to lose and they miss the mark. And perhaps this was the best way to shed her misconceptions and after forgetting all these misconceptions both of them hugged each other and started to prepare for the mission with a new zeal and enthusiasm.

13thOctober; Thursday

Niharika and Jasmine had already made the planning in the early morning. As directed she went onto the roof so that she couldn't be seen in the flat premises as even if by chance he got a doubt, all the planning will be ruined.

And as the time approached Niharika was waiting desperately for this highly awaited occasion.

This side even Jasmine was anxious that what would happen if he would not come? Her all planning will be ruined, her trap will go waste. Then she would have to wait for another few months. She was confident on her love trap but she was equally worried about the failure of her trap. And this side Mohit on his way was feeling happy. Finally he had got the chance for which he had aspired for more than three years. How desperately he wanted to sleep with his sex slave friend? He had tried a number of times but she didn't gave her any clue of more than friendship. Today he had brought an expensive gift item for her so that he can impress her at the first glance. How cleverly he had set the love trap that had made her feel that he loves her very much? He had made her so much insane in his love that she had herself invited him on her flat. Today he will have the best day in Jaipur. Today he will sleep with one of the hot chicks. Today he will not only sleep with her but will also make her understand that they can be in a live-in-relationship and will use her as a slave.

What an object this love is? A love in which both are setting trap for each other to fulfil their illegitimate aspirations.

The doorbell ranged and Jasmine hiding her emotions opened the gate.

"Happy Birthday darling! Happy Birthday." And Mohit hugged her tightly and kissed on her cheeks. Finding no protest he felt that today his dream is going to come true.

"Thank you baby! But why you are so late?"

"Oho! Baby. Sorry! I got late as I was purchasing a gift for you." And he presented her a beautiful golden ring.

"Oho! So sweet of you." She passed a wicked smile to him.

After the mandatory cake ceremony he greeted her happy birthday once again. Seeing no further move from Mohit, she threw the bait.

"You know Mohit; I used to love you since college. But you never cared for me in front of that witch. You were behind that damn Niharika."

"Its' not like that baby. I never loved that whore. You had heard na that she had multiple sex partners. I hate that name even. I love you and only you." He planted a soft kiss on her right cheek.

As Jasmine was eagerly waiting for this moment she also kissed him on his cheeks. After sometime they were kissing each other wildly. As the storm got over, Jasmine passed a satirical statement to Mohit which is almost unbearable for a guy at these moments and he would try his best to prove it wrong.

"Sweetheart! You are really an idiot. You don't know even how to please a girl. You don't know how to kiss a hot girl."

"Whattt???" Mohit was stammering and baffled at his stupidity of ruining his first impression and was unsure that what mistake he had made?

"Really! You don't know how to kiss a hot babe like me. Have you ever heard the 'Rope Kiss'; it's really interesting and seductive." She was passing satire on him regularly to let his morale down.

"I don't know." He was really feeling ashamed of his stupidity and ignorance about a kiss which he had thought the simplest task.

"You will tie my both hands to the two end of the bed and I will open my both legs and you will tie my both legs to the two ends of the bed and I will repeat the same thing on you and then only our lips would do the movement and we can enjoy the kiss as long as possible." She threw one more powerful bait this time.

"Really! Very romantic. Superb!"

And as it's the nature of boys that they feel aroused only if they hear the words that any girl is opening her both legs and Mohit was not an exception when Jasmine said him that she will open her legs. In fact he was feeling very much aroused and sensuality was running in his whole body.

Jasmine shed her shirt and jeans in front of him and Mohit was literally regretting on himself not to please such a hot babe.

"Ok! You open your clothes. I am bringing the ropes."

Mohit was feeling himself on the seventh sky after seeing Jasmine in almost a naked state. He was wondering that in a few moments even the remaining clothes would not be there on Jasmine's body and what a pleasant sight it would be? He will utilise all his knowledge to please this girl.

"Mohit! What are you doing? You haven't opened your shirt even. I am still confused when you tie me then you will not be able to tie yourself and will spoil my whole mood. You had already spoiled my mood one time." She was trying to take Mohit in her charm.

"Ok baby! I am opening my clothes. you can tie me firstly and then you can tie yourself. This time I will make you enjoy a lot."

Jasmine tied his hands and legs to all the four end of the bed.

"Now, how will you tie yourself baby? " Mohit was trying to be romantic.

"I will call my friend. She will tie me to the bed. Actually she has a crush on you. She wants to have some fun with you. Firstly we will enjoy and then I will tie her and please make her happy also."

Mohit couldn't believe on his ears. He wasn't still sure that how can he be so much lucky that he was going to get two hot chicks at the same time.

"C'mon baby! It's the time to enjoy." Jasmine passed the message to her friend.

But the girl who came downstairs, Mohit couldn't have dreamt even in his dreams. His eyes were not ready to believe the sight which he was seeing at this moment. He felt that someone had hit with him an iron rod. He understood that he had been trapped. He was speechless. His mind was still not accepting that it was Niharika Ahuja and how can she come here? But now thinking about these things were of no use. He had been totally trapped.

"Nihu! Tell him; what's the reward of betraying a girl and using her as a birthday party for your friends. Nihu! This is my birthday gift for you."

"I am sorry! I am really sorry! Please forgive me." Mohit was in total despair.

But for the first time this talkative Niharika was not in a mood to utter a single word. She picked his shirt and forced into his mouth so that he can't vise further craps. And she took his belt lying on the floor and started beating him like a madman. And when she became tired and found that still he is alive, she took the knife from the kitchen and slit down his veins whose blood had already drained up. And she pulled out the clothes from his mouth so that she can listen him moaning from pain. But he was so much drained up that he was moaning like a child. Even though she had taken an oath not to show even the slightest degree of pity towards this demon she felt some pity on him and slit down his neck and his pain and he himself was over permanently.

"Jasmine! I had done it."

"Congrats Nihu! Congrats! You had done it."

And they picked their luggage which had been already packed and went from there never to come back again to this flat or to this city.

Chapter-28

❁ ❁ ❁

Both the girls were very much happy when they were taking the final exit from the city of palaces. They had put down the foundation of their palace in such a grand way that they haven't even dreamt of? Obviously it had taken them almost a span of almost four months but this was of no concern as they had made themselves mentally prepared for the time which was going to elapse in their voyage of revenge. And when they reached to the Jaipur station there was no any sign of hastiness or such type of emotions which normally exist on a murderer's face which makes them suspected. Why they would display such type of emotions when they had not murdered any person, they have given a lesson to that knave who was scot-free from almost two years after committing such a monstrous crime. They are happy that they had made the work of the police departments and social reformers by eradicating them from the society who are not less than the curse for this so called civilized society. They were happy that they were returning to the base camp which they had selected as a destination for their planning. And that base camp was Niharika's house as this was the place which was enough for her not to lose her motivation in her expedition. And as they had already booked the ticket in advance they headed to their compartment and made them relax by ordering a coffee which they needed most at this time.

***

Once again a party was organised in Niharika's house to celebrate and discuss the further course of actions.

"Now what, Jasmine?"

"Obviously we would head for our next destination and will set the trap for our next goat."

"But Jasmine, we should firstly ponder upon the fact that what were the mistakes in our first murder and then we would consider upon the positive points from our murder so that our next move will be more careful."

After a brainstorming session, they once again made a list of what were the positive and negative factors in completing their project.

Negative Points

1. It took more time than expected.
2. We used our real names to call us even in public places
3. We joined a coaching institute which made us familiar with more persons.
4. We didn't destroyed the weapon in excitement.

5.   We got a coordination problem in mid-between of the project.

6.   We had used the trains as a means of communication which had let our fake names registered in govt. file which could create a problem for us in the long run.

7.   We had used our old laptops and cellphones which are registered under our originals names which we would have to dispose of.

8.   We had no internet connection and we used the cyber café which once again was a big blunder.

Positive Points

1.   It became successful.

2.   We didn't created any undue hassles.

3.   We didn't took the help of any outside member.

4.   We left the crime scene as possible.

5.   The use of fake ID in renting the flat and hotel helped us to save us from being suspected.

6.   We had tracked all the impostors with the help of our first victim.

7.   We have the address and contact number of all the impostors.

After listing the various negative points they tried to sort out all the possible negativity one by one. The very next day they brought two different laptops and mobiles from different shops and a Tata Photon+ for an internet connection as it didn't made them to buy one more fake simcard. And after few days after diagnosing any further loopholes they headed for Kanpur where there next target was residing.

Chapter-29

❋ ❋ ❋

Finally when they reached after a journey of almost five days by hiring different means of transportation, they were totally exhausted. They decided to book a room in Hotel Mandakini Palace and take rest for two days. Once when they were feeling refreshing again, they start to work upon their mission.

"Jasmine! How we are going to execute our plan?" Niharika started the string of the conversation.

"Actually, I am unable to decide that would be the same plan would be fine or we would have to innovate another thing." The sense of unsureness was glancing at Jasmine's face.

"I have a plan but a lot of risk is involved. As we had done our research, he works in a small company and as his salary is not so much impressive, he lives alone in a flat in Adarsh Nagar so that no one in the colony would know his real background and income. So I decided to send you alone and execute our plan?" There was a sense of confidence on Niharika's face.

"But Miss Nihu! How will I enter into his flat? Have you any plan regarding this and even if I enter in his flat, then how would I murder him? He will be extremely careful even if he would let me allow to enter his flat." She was quite puzzled at her friend's planning.

"That bastard had an appetite for sex and this lust is going to end his life." There was a sense of anger in Niharika's voice.

Even though Jasmine was not quite sure about the successfulness of this plan but she had enough confidence on Niharika. She was quite aware that her friend is so much better in devising a master plan for anything and she wished her good luck and said her to respond instantly as she would pass a missed call or a SMS in case any discrepancy happens.

***

Prakash was almost on her bed till now when he found the doorbell ranging. He was almost frowned to get interruption in his sleep as it was Sunday and this was the day for getting a nice sleep after a hell lot of work for the whole week. But as the doorbell was ringing continuously, he got up from the bed unwillingly and opened the door. But his whole sleep withered in a fraction of second when he saw Jasmine on the door.

"Happy Birthday Prakash! Many many happy returns of the day!"

"Thank you, thank you!" Even though Prakash was happy to get the first wish of his birthday, he was totally confused to find Jasmine at this unexpected hour.

"Prakash! Why are you having such a look on your face? If I am right, you are angry at my sudden interruption." Jasmine tried to look innocent.

"No! Its' not like that yar! Actually, I am confused that how you can be here when no one knows my address. I can understand that you would have known my birthday from fb but how can you get the address?" This side Prakash was using his common sense and power of reasoning and on the other side Jasmine was feeling disarmed with every passing moment without Niharika. She was such in a panicked state that she was fearful of getting her plan into limelight even before execution.

"Prakash! You are really mean. How willingly I had came to greet you happy birthday on such an early morning and in spite of calling me inside and giving a party for this feat you are questioning me like a criminal." She was trying to handle the situation with her full force having a false smile on her face.

"Oh! No yar! Its' not like that. Come! Come! Actually I am totally surprised at this unexpected surprise." Even till now Prakash was confused.

"You yourself had mentioned in your fb that you work in Quartz Technologies and my father had placed some graphic design offers from this company. I came to Kanpur for receiving the blueprint of these designs from the company and I was astonished in the same way as you are till now. But I am not mean like you that I would overreact. I asked your fellow colleagues and was in high spirits after finding a college mate in such a distant land. I hoped that you would feel happy after getting an unexpected surprise from my side, but I hope I was wrong." Jasmine whiplashed with her dose of satires which was as hollow as her story. In fact she was dying to tell that even though you had cut yourself from each and every one we had been able to locate you and now no one can save you. Even Jasmine was feeling contented after seeing the positive expressions on his face.

"Ok! Jasmine. I am really sorry. I am really really sorry! Change the topic. Now tell me what I should do in order to get the forgiveness from the young lady." Prakash was feeling baffled at his own stupidity and was trying hard not to get more embarrassment.

"Nothing much! Just a nice treat!"

It was just a matter of indication from the lady; Prakash spread the whole table with eatables which he had brought yesterday as he could at least arrange a small party to his closest friends.

"You are really a good guy. You had spread the whole table but its' like we are having a dinner not a birthday party!" Once again Prakash became the target of the lady's irony.

"Why what happened?" Prakash was feeling puzzled as he was unable to understand anything.

"Nothing! Perhaps you had hidden all the bottles and packets for your bachelor party." She once again fired her verbal weapon to take the control in her own hands.

"Its' not like that! I thought...Ok! I am coming in just a second." After it was just a matter of few seconds, the table was decorated with the bottles and packets which are today considered an important ingredient of any teenager's party. Even though the situation was under control after such a tough mind game with Prakash; Jasmine was in a total restless mood as she was not able to get any moment for the execution of her plan. Time was running fast and she was loathing herself for the wastage of the precious moments as it seemed that she was really enjoying the party. Then suddenly something erupted in her mind which she was wondering it as a master card.

"Prakash! Can I ask you a favour? Can you bring a bottle of beer for me as I don't feel contented just from wine?" She tried to pretend as she had been under the effect of wine and such demands are normal in such situations.

"Oh! Sure..." Prakash was also gradually travelling into a world of ecstasy.

As Jasmine was waiting for such moment, she very hastily mixed the sleeping-pills in his glass.

As expected, even few minutes wouldn't have passed; Prakash was in a different world of unconsciousness.

***

Finally when Prakash woke up almost after more than three hours, he was puzzled why and how he had been tied in ropes. It didn't take him a fraction of second to understand the whole situation when he saw both girls sitting on chairs. He understood that he had been trapped very badly.

"Prakash! Do you want to smoke a cigarette?" Jasmine passed a wicked smile to Niharika.

"I will not leave you bitches! I will not leave you." Prakash was shouting at the top of his voice.

Both of girls slapped them very hard and lighted a cigarette and offered him to smoke. And as he was helpless at this moment, he accepted the offer and started to smoke. But as his hands were bound he was not able to exhale the whole smoke and he started coughing but anyhow he faced this mortification which was just a humble reply of his lustful desires.

"Jasmine! What should we do when he is not fulfilling our orders?" Niharika tried to feel interrogative with Jasmine as she wanted a better solution of her problems.

"Bitch! I am doing as you are saying. Now how can I smoke the whole cigarette when my both hands are tied?" Prakash was shouting with the possible loudest voice which was in reality now just a groan of a puppy.

"Really! He can't smoke the whole cigarette. So why not we should make use of the remaining cigarette. Niharika! He had a very liking for blowjob, then why should his so called weapon would not smoke cigarette." Niharika cruel eyes were crystal clear of her intentions and each and every word of the beauty was raising a storm of fear in that bastard's heart. Before even Jasmine could analyze the situation, her friend had already unzipped the trousers of that felonious rascal and thrashed the remaining cigarette in his organ. The intensity of voice had Prakash would be in a normal situation was enough to alert the whole locality. As someone had said; "Each moment is a different moment." And today it was a different day. Even Jasmine was literally shocked at this incident as it was not a part of their plan but she could understand the thought-process of her friend at this point of time. This moment was the moment of vengeance of Niharika and she was not going to leave it. With each another cigarette it was almost becoming impossible to face this ordeal and he was feeling a high degree of suffocation and burning pain in his organ. His eyes became red and his whole body was trembling with rage. But they were not in a mood to leave him. And when it was literally impossible for him to bear this ordeal further; he became mortally unconscious as the burn marks with each and every moment was getting very high rather more than unbearable. Even though they had given him his desired punishment they pressed his Adam's apple till the time they became assured that the life of that salacious impostor had came to an end.

Both girls went from there to their hotel and left the city forever not to come again.

Once again the so called birthday had became death day for someone.

Chapter-30

❖ ❖ ❖

Both the girls were so much happy that their flair happiness doesn't knew any boundaries. They had the perfect reason to be happy as this task had been almost completed in a very small period of time. They had been able to murder the second bastard and they were not even being suspected for the first murder. They were aware of the fact that they had only just crossed the second milestone of their journey and a lot of there was to come. This time as they hadn't packed their luggage, they packed their impedimenta and checked out from the hotel. Once again without wasting a single second they headed towards the base camp. And as usual they arranged the home party and once again they were discussing upon the positive and negative points in completing this task.

Positive Points

1. It became successful.
2. It took very less time.

3. It took very less money to complete the task.
4. It was wonderful that we didn't leave any trail which can make us suspected.
5. We were able in not making any unnecessary contacts.

Negative Points

1. It was a very risky plan which had high chances of getting failed.
2. We are always using the kitchen knife as our weapon. Although we had disposed the knife into the toilet chamber but if we continue to use it could create a pattern which can make us suspected.
3. We had no any alternative plan in case of emergency.
4. If we try to be honest we are extra sure regarding our plans.
5. We had no any modern weapons in case of any emergency.
6. We had again booked a cheap hotel which can once again act as a pattern.

And after discussing upon the negative points they were finding ways to sort it out. The biggest problem was to purchase a modern weapon as it was not a commodity which can be brought from any normal shop. As they were not able to find a person who could help them in purchasing the weapons they were becoming restless with each passing day. But after a lot of research they were able to find a person who agreed to provide her the weapons from the black market on a condition of paying even more than rate which was prevalent in the black market. They agreed readily and paid 1, 25,000 for two pistols and 50,000 separately for hundred bullets. But then something happened which forced them to think again and again upon their master plan.

"Hey, Jasmine had you heard anything?" Ruchi, their common friend was almost in a shocked state as anyone could imagine from her voice.

"What happened?" Jasmine was terror-stricken as she didn't want to be interrupted by any another catastrophe.

"Don't you know, that Mohit and Prakash had been brutally murdered and this had been done perhaps by Niharika as they were involved in the gang rape?" Her voice was full of impending fear.

"OMG! How did this happened?" Jasmine was speaking in such a way that she had gone hysterical but Niharika was smiling at the way her friend was acting.

"Really! Abhishek's girlfriend Neha who is also my friend was telling that his boyfriend was telling him that his two friends of the previous college had been murdered. And Abhishek got to know this when one day he had some work with Prakash and he didn't get any response. Wondering that he would have gone to his house, he called at his home; he was almost in a terror when he found that his friend had been very brutally murdered 15 days before. And when he called his all friends to share this tragic news, he found that Mohit had been also murdered very brutally and that even almost one month before. You know Jasmine, I think that except Niharika no one can murder them brutally as people say that she was gang raped very brutally and she is taking her revenge. I am also confident because she was very good in planning. But some people say that she is in a mental asylum and some people say that she had committed suicide. God knows, but I am very fearful. I am only telling you because you are the only whom I can trust. And if both murders are not just a coincidence then Niharika will not leave anyone who will come in their way. I am really fearing and I will also suggest you not to be in contact with her. Do you know where is she residing this time?" Ruchi explained everything in a row.

"No. I am not in contact with her after that incident."

And after some normal talks both wished a good bye to each other.

For the first time Jasmine was feeling herself on an advantageous position as she had got the desired piece of news without any setbacks and failure of her plans. Perhaps it would have been the first case where a girl had been benefitted by a girl's weakness. As it is a girl's nature that she can't digest any secrets and Ruchi had explained everything in detail in a row without inquiring anything which had helped to reframe their plan in a different way.

Both girls understood a simple fact after this conversation that they are scared and had become aware and careful. And it was almost impossible for them to stick upon their old methods of setting the trap by giving them a chance to have sex with either of them and then murdering them.

"Now, Niharika what should we do? My mind is not working. You would have to think something brilliant which would not get failed."

"What is there to think? The person who had told us this news will help us in completing our task."

"Are you silly? Why will Ruchi help us?"

"I am not talking about Ruchi. That rogue's girlfriend will help us. I can't let him destroy any other innocent girl's life."

"But how will Neha help us?"

"I will let that innocent girl to know the facts which she is unaware of about that specious demon and we will ask for her help. If she will refuse, we will firstly motivate her and if she agrees then it is fine and as Ruchi had told you that no one will live who come in our mission." There was a sense of confidence in Niharika's eyes.

And Jasmine was quite satisfied as she could see the fire of revenge and concern for an innocent girl's life in Niharika's eyes.

Chapter-31

❖ ❖ ❖

After a brainstorming session of almost two days they headed for their new destination. And this new destination was not a new place for them. This was the place where Niharika had came with new aspirations, dreams and God knows what more. And this was the place which once was filled with her charm and bubbliness was now a haunted place for her. She didn't wanted even to set her foot in its premises. But Jasmine made her understand that she would have to overcome these emotional barriers as it would create hindrance in their mission. But how would a girl's heart make herself understand that the origination of this mission is due to this cursed place. But a human being is a slave of circumstances and understanding this basic philosophy of life she agreed to put her foot on the soil of Pune.

As usual they booked a room in a hotel but this time the hotel was quite expensive. This hotel was The Oakwood Premiere which was one of the premiere hotel of Pune. Finally after taking a caldarium they sat for discussing the further plan in the early morning.

"Nihu! As we know that Abhishek is studying here in MBA in our college and Neha is also in same class. So we would have to firstly focus on Neha as her support would make our work easy. But in case the bad fate will continue to haunt us and Neha forbids to help us, then we will kill Neha and I will go to the university directly and I kill him as soon as possible." Jasmine explained the plan in detail.

"That's the perfect plan. You will go firstly to market to purchase a burqa and in the mean time I am creating a fake ID by the name of any non-hindu and you will go in burqa so that there would be no any problem at the time of entrance or exit. And one thing more, call Neha and say her that you are Ruchi's friend and call her in the hotel." Niharika corrected the plan by suggesting some recommendations.

As Niharika started to prepare a fake ID under the name of Shajia Akhtar in the meantime Jasmine called Neha.

"Am I speaking to Neha Sinha?"

"Yes! Who are you?"

"I am Jasmine Backefield; Ruchi's friend and she had given your number. (But the reality was that they had arranged her number from the college directory after a lot of hassles.) Listen to me carefully and then say anything. Ruchi told me that you have told him about the murder of Prakash and Mohit and Abhishek is also so much scared and as you are Abhishek's girlfriend, you would never want that he would be murdered. I have something to tell you which could save your boyfriend's life. And as he is also my friend I also want to save him but I can't do it alone. As I have came from Indore just to meet you when Ruchi told me all these things. You can come to the hotel as soon as possible. I would have met directly to Abhishek but the murderer is keeping an eye on him and I didn't wanted to be in limelight and that's why I had called you. And you also take care that you don't meet even with Abhishek as I had told you that the murderer is keeping a strict eye on Abhishek, you may also be murdered. So if you want to save Abhishek, meet me as soon as possible for having a tote-a-tote as I will return just in the evening as I don't want to die." Jasmine created the atmosphere of fear and terror for Neha without taking a pause.

"I am coming. I am coming…." She started to stumble sensing the impending disaster. And after disconnecting the phone she didn't even care what she was wearing and she headed for the hotel.

Oh! How much pure the teenage love is? A teenager is so much engrossed in the love of his amant that he do not consider that what is right or wrong where his beloved happiness is at stake. He do not even pay a slight attention to the fact that is anyone trying to cheat him on his sweetheart's name or there is reality in what that particular person is saying. A teenager takes care of this virtue so much that he is ready to put his life at stake if his soulmate is going to be happy and in a well-being condition.

And when Neha ranged the doorbell, Jasmine opened the door to welcome her. Neha greeted both of the girls being unknown of the fact that they were the murderer themselves.

"Neha! Do you want to know that who is the coupe jarret of Mohit and Prakash? " Jasmine broke the ice as there was almost silence after they had wished each other.

"Yes!" She nodded her head in affirmative.

"Do you want to know that who is keeping a strict eye on your boyfriend and is going to murder him today only?"

Neha was so much terror-stricken that she couldn't manage to utter any word. She felt as it was the last chance to save her boyfriend.

"We are the murderers and we are going to kill your Abhishek today." Both girls declared the secret to her in unison.

What would she say to both of the girls? Her mind got blocked as whom she had considered an angel was demon. And she had made a bevue already by coming here to the hotel instead of informing Abhishek. She felt that she had been an easy prey of these dames de la halle. But she tried to make a last attempt to save her boyfriend. As its' the nature of management students that they try to handle any situation by the help of the motivational thoughts and quotes as they are taught that motivation has so much power that it can alter a person's decision.

"I know that when you have decided to kill my boyfriend, you will surely kill him and will not listen any request from my side. But will you even give me the privilege of knowing the cause which had propelled you to take his life. Even the God asks for the last wish of the dying person and when you are going to murder him, actually you are beheading my soul. So can you fulfil my last wish of getting to the cause which had bonded the enmity to such an extent that you two friends are adamant on killing him? And if I would find the reasons justified, I am giving a process verbal that I will myself help you to murder him and if the reasons are weak and you are the so called cultured people then its' your wish how you want to continue?" Neha threw the bait so that she can delay the time and can make their plan unsuccessful.

And both girls unaware of this fact described her each and every detail what compelled them to kill those felonious creatures and why they are going to kill her amant.

"I would like to say something after listening this tragic saga and let me complete before you would take any steps."

Both girl replied in affirmative in hope of getting support from her.

"I am really sorry to hear this that this type of ordeal you had to go through. I can understand that what you would have been feeling from the moment you had encountered this tragedy. It is very wrong that a girl is used as an object of enjoyment, humiliation, lust and a hell lot of things. I am also a girl and I couldn't have left such type of pusillanimous butchers who had committed such a heinous crime willingly. How can a person be so much heartless that he will treat us an object. Are we objects who are made just for their pleasure?" Both girls were smiling in their sub-conscious mind as everything was happening according to the plan as they had expected.

She continued her conversation after drinking a glass of water.

"But I can't understand a very simple fact that when you had been betrayed by your own boyfriend, why you are behind my boyfriend? It was the fault of your so called boyfriend who had seen as you a sex slave from the very first day you would have befriended him. It was your fault that you do not have even the basic etiquette to know the difference between a good boy and a specious fellow. And if the other boys raped you on the direction of your so called boyfriend, it was his fault and not of that boys. If any boy would get a chance to fuck a girl, he will never forbid. If today Abhishek invites his own friends to rape me, it would be his fault and not theirs. And if I would be so much insane that I would take an oath to take revenge, then I will not take the revenge from all the boys, instead I will take revenge from Abhishek. It is your stubbornness and frustration which is compelling you to take revenge. Even when you would ponder upon this fact with a cool mind then you will find that you are just creating an avernus for yourself once again by taking the curse of those families whose family members you are murdering. I am sorry to say that none of the guys except your Mohit had seen you ever with bad eyes but it was your Mohit who welcomed them to serve you as a sex slave for them. I don't know about all the guys but I can bet upon Abhishek that he is not the guy which you are thinking. I am in relationship with him from more than one year and not a single moment had came when he did anything which could hurt me. I know that you are not listening it carefully but I would say that you are not taking revenge you are only pouring out the frustration of Mohit on other guys. Niharika, even retreat this time and live a new life which is awaiting for you.

And you Jasmine! Tell me only one thing that on what background you are supporting her? I can understand that you are her best friend and you helped him in the time of need but which type of help is this that you are supporting her to commit crime. Which type of friend are you that firstly you help her and in lieu of helping her you are pushing her into a great dungeon from where she wouldn't be able to escape. I am sorry to say that if I were in your place, I would have make her understand not to make her hands dirty with criminal activities. I would have helped her to set a new life. And how much generous you are that is even beyond my imagination. You try an old technique of calling me in the hotel and then say me to support you to kill my own boyfriend. I didn't come here as I was so much badaud that I can't understand such type of tricks, instead I came here as I have the genuine love for Abhishek. You talked about betrayal in love and you are saying me to betray my own love. You yourself say to me how I can help you when you even being a friend is walking on your friend's footsteps and I should ditch my own love. Jasmine! Please leave these things and take your friend to the better path of life and help her to give her life a new meaning." Neha had almost given a speech to these girls.

She was feeling that she had almost brainwashed them and she was almost successful in saving her boyfriend. But hardly had she an idea that these girls were mature enough not to get distracted by reverse motivation which Neha was trying to inject in these girls?

"Finished your part?" Both girls asked in a satirical tone.

"Yes! Now what is your decision to kill him or not?" She asked with a sense of confidence.

Both girls shot her together in her head with their newly purchased weapons.

***

Jasmine put on the burqa which she had purchased at Niharika's direction. She was wondering why people criticize such a beautiful dress. Why people bluntly satire on the girls who wear this nice piece of clothes? And when she glanced in the mirror she was feeling a sense of pride on her beaux yeaux. She wondered how she can be so much ignorant of the beauty of her eyes? It was all the generosity of this dress that had made aware of her beautiful brown eyes. And looking once again in the mirror and patting herself for the task, she headed towards the university. She was quite surprised to find that for the first time the huissier didn't ask about her identity-card before entering the college. She was feeling pleased at the magic of the dress as it was the charm of the dress which didn't let the huissier dare to ask her identity. As it is a common phenomenon in our society that we tend to have a mindset about the girl wearing burqa is that she would be a genuine girl having a high degree of respect of her character. People didn't even try of eve-teasing on her as they are considered girl of high moral value and respect towards her family and society. Jasmine taking the advantage of this mindset entered into the college.

She went into the bathroom and changed her dress and came to her original form and dialled the number of Abhishek and called her in the canteen. Abhishek was a little-bit surprised to find Jasmine at this point of time in the college but they wished each other. And after few normal conversations, when Abhishek asked about the reason of Jasmine to come into the college, she replied:

"Ruchi told me that you are in danger of being murdered and I know the reason and the person who wants to murder you."

Abhishek was literally shocked to hear this piece of news from Jasmine and he was not in a situation to say anything. But anyhow he cleared his throat.

"Who is that person and why does he want to kill me Jasmine?" His every word was full of terror.

"Should I explain here or can we talk in private at least?" She threw the bait towards him.

"No! No! We will go to some private place. Let's go." The fear of being dead is so much gracious that a person loses his power of reasoning.

And they went to the park of the college and sat behind the bushes as they were couples so that no one can see them in due course of their conversation.

"Now please tell me Jasmine, who is that mother-fucker who wants to kill me and why the fuck does he wants to kill me?"

"You remember Niharika Ahuja! She wants to kill you and I think you better know the reasons." She said with a fake tenderness in her voice.

After listening Niharika's name everything became quite crystal clear in front of his eyes. Even a layman could clearly spectacle the repent and terror in his eyes at the same time. But before he could speak anything he was almost in a shocked state to see a pistol directed towards him. And before he could think anything further, the pistol had done its work and Abhishek became a history.

Jasmine went up from there directly to the washroom and changed her clothes. And once glancing at her beautiful eyes in the mirror she came out of the gate without being interrupted. From there she went to the hotel where Niharika was desperately waiting for her friend.

And once again without making any further delay, they checked out from the hotel and started to return to their base camp.

Chapter-32

❋ ❋ ❋

The next morning whole Pune came to a stand-still seeing the newspaper headlines. A girl had been shot dead in one of the best hotels of Pune and the so called temple of education, the Symbiosis University was labelled as a shelter of criminals where a boy was shot dead in spite of such a high degree of safety which the college management claims. Each and every newspaper was flooded with the news of these two murders. And not only the college management but also the hotel owner were unable to give reply of any of the questions of the media which were regularly whiplashing them with their comments and questions.

"Sir, how can anyone enter into college when you have a strict security system?"

"Sir, what would have been the reason that the murderer had chosen your college for giving his act a final touch?"

"Were you aware that this is going to happen in your college?"

"Had any outsider killed your student or anyone from the inside had done this work?"

"Is there the case of any affaire d'amour that the victim had been killed?"

"How can parents assure their wards in your college?"

These were just a few ardentia verba of the lot which was regularly asked by the college management which they were failing to answer as they had themselves hardly an idea that happened into their college.

But the real sufferer was the hotel owner who not only loses his customer base instantly but also was getting regularly attacked by the media reporters.

"Sir, how can anyone intrude in your hotel premises when there is such a high degree of security?"

"Is any sex racket was running in your hotel?"

"Do the terrorists take shelter in your hotel and the poor girl unfortunately listened their conversation and was shot dead?"

"You are saying that they came with a fake ID and they were girls. Then are you not trying to hide something as it seems impossible that two girls come with their fake ID just for murdering a girl?'

"Was there any nexus between the staffs of the hotel in this crime?"

"Is it true that your some staff tried to do something wrong with the girl and she committed suicide and you shot her dead to save your hotel's reputation?"

The hotel owner was almost in a hysterical situation from the questions as he had made his hotel not only a safe destination for the tourists but had also saved it from the pollutions of the hotel line.

***

The police department was almost in a shocked state after two consecutive murders on the same day and both in the high-profile destinations of the city. One was a popular destination for the students from all over India and it was not such a college where everyone can take admission. It was the destination where the children of optimates used to get their education. And the other one was one of the costliest hotels of the city which only high-class Super-Rich persons can afford. But the biggest concern was that there was enough pressure on the police department as both organisation wanted to catch the culprit as soon as possible as their image was tarnishing. But even after initial investigations, they were unable to find any concrete reason for the murder, leave the possibility of finding the murderers. And the information which they had got after first hand interrogation had made the situation more complex. They got almost concrete information that both Abhishek Kishore and Neha Sinha were couples. The case of honour killing was almost negligent as both families were totally unaware of their relationship but even though they were not denying the possibility. And when the primary officer was unable to find any clue he demanded help from the higher authority and they handed the case to the S.P; Mr. Aditya Khanna who was notorious for having a very ruthless approach towards criminals.

Chapter-33

❊ ❊ ❊

Santosh and Rajesh when heard that even Abhishek had been murdered were really scared as they were unsure how much they are going to live more. They were not able to get any idea which could save them. They were repenting on what had they had done but there was no use of crying over spilt milk. They were sure that they are not going to live. They were clueless that whom of them is going to meet its undeserved end first and they were living in fear. They had not committed any culpa levis that they can discuss even with the best of their well-wishers and this was their main concern. If they had to remain alive they had to do something themselves. They will have to fight alone for being alive with their own con silio et animis. They were living their life in terror to such an extent that they always wondered that each and every place and people in this world are framing a conspiracy for their murder. Even the homes in which they were residing far from their house were like a haunted place for them. They were not able to assess any way in which how could they make themselves safe from their unexpected death. The condition in which they were living did not allow them to return their home as the fear of death was crystal clear on their face. They had almost made up their mind then suddenly an idea stroked in Rajesh mind which gave him a chance to save him from this ordeal. And without making any pause he dialled the number of Santosh.

This side Santosh was so much fear-stricken so much that he was avoiding every call except his parents. And it took Rajesh to wait for almost twenty missed calls to get Santosh on line.

"Hii Santosh! How are you?"

Santosh felt a sigh of relief to hear the voice of Rajesh as he thought that someone else is calling from his mobile and he had been murdered.

"Thank God! You are here. I thought…" It was the terror of these two girls that even when one of them was asking about the other's well-being, the other one was asking he is alive or not.

"I am in very much terror. But I have got a brilliant idea which could perhaps save us." He paused to get any response from other end but alas! The other one was also equally in terror and he didn't want to interrupt when he was talking about how to be safe. And understanding his thought-process Rajesh continued.

"One thing I notice that she is murdering each one of us alone and we are two in number. If we unite together and make a counter-plan, then we both can save ourselves. And one thing more, I had noticed that she is making the campo santo of our those friends who were in north India and if this is not a coincidence, I am her next target. And that's why I had called you to please help me in this period of distress. I need your help so that we can teach her a lesson once again. She is in an advantageous position as we are far from each other and this is making her powerful. If we got united, it will make her weak and we can save each of our own lives."

Santosh was feeling a sense of peace when he found out that he is not their next target. He replied him in affirmative and after disconnecting the call he was now at least less fearful. Even though he had replied him in affirmative he was sure that he was not going to help him as he didn't wanted to be the next corpse instead of Rajesh. In the meantime he found a very strong coincidence that each and every one was murdered as they were out of their home and he decided to get back to his home.

What an irony! This side Jasmine was so much faithful to her friend that she had put her whole life at stake for her friend's happiness and this side Santosh was so selfish that he had refused to help his friend whose life was in danger. How does the fear of death make a person selfish, one would have understood if he would have a look at Santosh thought-process.

Chapter-34

❧ ❧ ❧

And once again after arranging a home party they sat down to scribble the negative and positive points which they had observed after completing their third task. When almost after a discussion of half an hour they got to know that only they had done one thing wrong. The only Himalayan blunder committed by them was the murder of Neha Sinha which was not intended prima facia. (They had became hot topic of each and every newspaper which they were not still considering a mistake.) And the positive aspect of this task was that they had used silencer on their pistols which helped them to get away from being suspected. But hardly they had an idea that they have been unknowingly been on the hit-list of S.P; Aditya Khanna.

Finally when the discussion turned to the planning section, they were feeling a lot of problem. As the discussion now emphasized on the fact that the murder of the rest impostors had become quite tough as they had sensed that they are getting killed one by one on a random basis without any secundum ordinem. And they now could go to the police for protection as everyone loves their own life.

But their instinct said that they will not go to the police as they committed such a heinous act that if they will reveal themselves in front of police they will not only lose their image but they can also get a death penalty and this thought made them secure. This side they marked Santosh as their next target unaware of the counter-plan of those two guys. Now when they sat together to have research on Santosh, they got to know some facts which were quite shocking. He was not only the spoilt child of a rich brat but he had not left the lust of sex even though his friends were murdered one by one. But after the news of the murder of his third friend, he was very much careful and it was almost impossible for them to make a prey of him. They were not getting any idea how to get in touch with him. And as these girls had selected Santosh as their next target, they were adamant to murder him first. The days were passing but they had till now maintained the decorum of being patient to avoid any false move.

As it had been said that even though a criminal is wise enough, he leaves a clue which ruin their plan. And even after a lot of brainstorming these girls failed to understand that they had selected all the victims which were residing in north India and this had given the guys an opportunity to make a counter-plan collectively but really the plan was on individual basis. But Santosh unaware of the fact that these girls were not alone like him and they were choosing their target on a random basis and they had reached his doorsteps. He didn't have the slightest idea they were far ahead of him in planning and he was under strict surveillance even before he got the idea of going back to his home.

***

How sometimes a person's lust transforms into final wish, a person could have understood if he would have read the mind of Santosh. As Santosh was scared to be killed, he was not able to concentrate his mind on anything else. And as he was the vaurien of a rich brat, he was one of the few spoilt students of this world who took the student life as an opportunity to enjoy the life to the ultima thule whether it would be a legitimate or illegitimate form of enjoyment. And his lust for sex was so much that he used to utilise his parent's hard-earned money on call-girls. And as he was till now still sure that his days are over and he has very few days left and now when he was going to home for forever, he wanted to fulfil his lust for the last time as he could be murdered anytime. But perhaps he had the slightest idea that his this lusty habit been noticed by that girls and they have set a trap for him there also. And what an irony of nature that a person never follow the same pattern when he is doing some good things but he always follow the same pattern when he commits any wrong thing. And as these girls have forecasted he booked a call girl from the same agency for the next night.

"Mam, your fiancée had booked two girl for today's' night." The owner of the agency informed Jasmine. But hardly that lady had an idea that she was not doing any such thing which she can treat as virtue. Instead of this unknowingly she is partnering in the murder of a guy who is already scared. But how can a person know what is running in other person's mind. Jasmine had told her that as Santosh is her fiancée and she suspects that he is a characterless guy and she wants to catch him red-handed so that she can save her life from being pushed into hell. Jasmine had not only requested from that lady but also promised her to give a handsome amount of money to save her life and her avenir being pushed into darkness. And as it's the human psychology that when your hands are dipped into the activities which made you labelled as nasty in the society, you want to perform such things desperately which are termed as humane activities. And as we have been taught from our childhood that to save a girl or a woman's life from being spoilt is the biggest virtue and is not less than a blessing of God, the lady promises to fulfil her promises.

"Thank you. You will only send one girl." And the sense of victory was glancing at Jasmine's face.

"Ok Mam! I understood everything."

It is a well-known fact that excess of everything is bad. But perhaps the excess lust of Santosh would prove so much heavy on him, he couldn't have dreamt in his dreams. Even though these girls had made once again a risky plan for entering into Santosh flat, his excessive lust made their work easier as now the one of the call-girl was no one other than Niharika.

***

Oh! When will this girl come? This agency always gives tension to me. I had told them a number of times that I love punctuality but why they behave in such an unprofessional manner, I can't understand. They should understand that a person gets only six to eight hours of enjoyment at the cost of such a huge money. They should take care of our money. I understand they send hot chicks in lieu of our money but why they do not understand that a man wants to spend more time with hot chicks. Oh! How much will be today's night wonderful. I would get a coup de hassard of enjoying two babes at the same time and I will able to shed all the tension which this damn Niharika had given me from last few days. Due to this bitch, I am not able to even sleep properly. But today I will enjoy the whole night and in the morning, I will get on the train for my home. Then I will only see how this whore can murder me? I will kill her even if by chance I get a glance of her. What does she think that unlike that badaud guys she can kill me the way she wants?

The doorbell ranged and he was exclaimed to see an extremely hot girl but was equally surprised to see one of them in burqa. He was feeling a sense of uneasiness as one of the girl was in sensual western clothes and other was in extreme traditional clothes.

"Why are you wearing such type of clothes?" He asked in a frowned tone and hearing no reply from her he was wondering that this is the reason that the city like Madurai will always remain behind and can't develop like a metro city.

"Sir, this is her first time and she is feeling awkward." The other girl replied.

And Santosh hearing the fact that it's her first time felt aroused as its' the nature of boys that they feel a sense of ecstasy when they get to know that they are going to get a virgin girl.

"Ok! Come inside. And get ready as it's already late. I am going to the washroom." He was ordering them in a commanding tone.

But the sight which he witnessed after coming from the washroom was not less than a nightmare for him. This was Niharika and he had been trapped. But even before he could speak something he was shot dead. And the girl adjoining her was almost hysterical and terror was reflecting as she hadn't expected it the least.

"Don't worry. I have nothing to do with you." She handed her a bundle of notes before retiring from the crime scene.

Once again the lust had taken one more life.

Chapter-35

❧ ❧ ❧

What would have been the thought-process of Rajesh at the time when he found that Santosh had been murdered and he was their last target, it needs no explanation? He was so much terrorised by these girls that even he was not able to sleep for a single fraction of a second. He started to feel that the girls are coming and going to murder him at any point of time. The ghost of Niharika was haunting him to such an extent that he used to cry at midnight. He was not getting any clue that how he can save himself? He was wondering that why he had committed such a blunder by coming in the words of Mohit that he is now almost in articulo mortis. He was so much fearful that his only hope was the God who can save his life. He was regularly praying or better say begging in front of God to save his life. But if God would have started saving the life of these morons then hadn't He been blamed for being partial. And finding no clue to save his life, he decided something which could ruin his career but can save his life. And as it has been said that life is more precious than anything else, he decided to ruin his image but at least to save his life.

***

And when he reached home, his parents were literary shocked in which their child had reached. It seemed that he hadn't ate anything from many days. He was not the normal guy who reflected a sense of charm on his face. The sense of terror and fear was crystal clear on his face. And as it had been said that a father can understand his son better, it was not possible to hide that Rajesh is in a state of terror. Not only his this ordeal but also ghost of Niharika was not leaving him in his home also. He used to start crying at the midnight and uttering "Peccavi! Peccavi! But I do not want to die, papa; I do not want to die." And it was such an ordeal for his parents that their son is in such a panic state that his life is in danger. But how could a parent forecast that what his or her son had committed sin which is compelling him to die at an age which he can't even dream of. And when this ordeal continued for the second day his father decided to know the reason why his son is in such a terror. Or there is any reason that had anyone threatened due to his enmity with any person.

And the next morning, when Mr. and Mrs. Khatri called his son and asked the reason, Rajesh was feeling blushed and his head was mourned in shame. How could he tell his parents that he had committed a sin and he deserved such type of punishment? Even though he had decided that he will tell his parents the whole truth but he was not able to gather so much courage. But the ghost of Niharika had terrorised him so much that he is not at peace in his own house. It was almost unable to hide this secret as his one thought said that if he would hide this secret for a long time, he will lose his life. And he decided to reveal the secret and save his life.

"Papa! I want to make a confession. I had committed a sin but I don't want to die. I don't want to die. Please save me papa! Please save me."

"Relax my child! Nothing will happen to you as far as I am with you. Tell me what happened." He tried to put his son at ease.

"Papa! How can I say you that your child is such a moron who doesn't deserve to be called your son but I don't want to die?" Even the words of his father was not giving him comfort.

"Tell me my son. We will save you from any problem. We will save you. Keep trust on us." Mrs. Khatri tried to assure her son.

"Mom! It is a long story back. It's almost more than two years when there was the birthday of one of my friend. And he had a girlfriend who used to love her very much but he didn't cared at all. And on the eve of birthday he called her in his flat to have sex with her. And he also invited four friends including me so that we can have enjoyment with her. And we went from there as we found it a grand opportunity to have enjoyment. And we had a gang rape with that girl for the whole night. And not only we raped her but also tortured her brutally. And after this incident, we almost forgot that incident as she left the college and we thought she had either committed suicide or had done something. But she is back and killing us one by one. She had killed all the four of us and now only I am remaining. But I don't want to die. I know that I had done a very nasty work for which I can't even ask forgiveness from you but please save me. I do not want to die. Please, please..." He confessed almost all things in a row before he broke into tears.

Mr. and Mrs. Khatri were almost speechless and they themselves broke into tears when they heard their son's nasty activity. Their head were literally down with shame and remorse. They were feeling guilty on themselves for not giving them him the proper upbringing and 'Sanskar' which could make their child a source of pride for them. Leave the pride; they were such cursed parents that their child had brought such a degree of shame for them that they felt they have been stabbed from back by their own child. They were wondering what crime they had committed that they had been cursed being called the parents of such a nasty child. But as it has been said that for a parent the child will always remain his child even though he commits any wrong thing, sin, virtue; it doesn't matter for them. And with tears in their eyes, they tried to console their son at the time when consolation for Rajesh was almost like oxygen from them.

"Nothing will happen my dear Rajesh! We will save you." Even though they were unsure why they want to save such a demon and why they are giving shelter to such a demon.

Rajesh was now not in a situation to say anything and he was feeling light-hearted after confessing as someone had removed a burden from his heart. After seeing his parents in tears he was himself feeling culprit in his own eyes. And when he sensed that they were weeping more severely whenever they had a glance at his face, he went from there repenting on his fate and his deeds. And when Mr. and Mrs. Khatri tears dried after such degree of lamenting, they were in terror that how they could save their child? They were not a teenager unlike Rajesh who could underestimate the situation. Mr. Khatri and Mrs. Khatri both being a lecturer of psychology of a reputed college could understand the thought-process of a serial killer who is motivated by the feeling of revenge. And this thing was a major concern for them as she was not any serial killer who is a person of diseased mentality or a serial killer who is taking revenge from the whole world as her childhood was so much disastrous and she is a victim of inferiority complex. And their whole day went in either cursing themselves or thinking about their son's fate.

Chapter-36

✦ ✦ ✦

"Niharika; how will you murder Rajesh? He had been extremely careful after all these murders and he had returned to his home. But there is one thing important that his home is also in Indore and this could be beneficial for us." Jasmine was almost in a worried state.

"Does he knows that you are from Indore and you are with me?" Niharika was asking something important but her mind was somewhere else.

"He knows that I am from Indore but he doesn't know that I am with you except Backefield uncle."

"Backefield will not open his mouth as he is not only an etourdi but also a greedy chap. And one thing more, there is nothing to worry. I will manage everything."

"But how?" There was a sense of exclamation on Jasmine's face.

"It's your hometown and not any terra incognita where you will find difficulty. It will be easiest of all the tasks."

"Ok Nihu! You book a room in the Fortune Landmark which is not only almost 5km from the Lakshmi Bai Nagar

Railway Station but also at a distance of about 15km via Eastern Ring Road where my home is situated."

"Ok!"

And then Niharika explained him in detail how they will execute their plan.

***

"Hey my son! Welcome! How long it had been to see you?" Jasmine's mother was happy to see her daughter back to her home after such a long time and both of them hugged each other.

"Yes! Mom, you know na; how much the jobs are taxing in nature? I didn't get time."

"Had you informed us, your father would have come to the station to receive you." Mrs. Backefield words were full of care.

"I wanted to give you a surprise." And she passed a fake smile to her mother.

Both mother and daughter went inside the house to start a string of conversations which can normally be expected from two females. The evening was a period of grand celebration for the Backefield family. But even in the midst of these celebrations Jasmine mind was somewhere else.

The following morning she went around the whole city to have a close look at her city which was quite transformed in the last six months. After resting in her home for a week she invited Niharika to come to her city. And Niharika once again booked a hotel for her residence and to plan the further things.

If there would have been an instrument which can measure the level of commitment in a relation, 90% of the problems of the world would have ceased to exist. The same girl whom even the angels of God would have appreciated for the level of commitment towards her friend would have been literally shocked to find that the same girl is ditching one friend for fulfilling the commitment to another friend. People say that the childhood friends are closer to our heart than the friend whom we get in the later stage of our life. But perhaps these things mattered least to Jasmine otherwise she wouldn't have used Sakshi as a weapon for setting the trap for her own brother. And poor Sakshi unaware of these philosophical insights accepted the Jasmine's invitation to go for a movie. Had she had an idea that she would become the reason of her brother's death she would have never accepted.

Jasmine and Sakshi went to the mall to enjoy the movie which Sakshi was hardly aware that it was a trap. She was enjoying the movie thoroughly and Jasmine was finding the right moment to proceed her plan. And in this fix when the three hours came to an end both of them were unable to assess. While Sakshi was in a very good mood, Jasmine was equally frowned as time was running out. Then something clicked in Jasmine's mind which made her delighted. She asked Sakshi to wait and she herself went to the washroom.

"Hey Rajesh! I am Jasmine. Are you hearing me?"

"Yes! Tell me what happened?"

"I don't know whether you will believe me or not but I want to tell you something."

Rajesh was once again fearful sensing any impending danger.

"Sakshi and I had come to the mall for a movie as you know. Sakshi was talking to some boy named Aanand that as she is with me; she will come to the old fort after the movie. She was saying that she will only give kiss to her this time and rest things some other day. Look Rajesh; as you and Sakshi both are my friend, I told you but don't tell Sakshi that I told you. You are understanding na! Ok! Bye. Sakshi is waiting for me." Jasmine was feeling wonderful as the trap had been set.

Rajesh disconnected the call wondering what had happened to him that new problem are sprouting every day. Had it been any other day he would have been full of rage and would have taken an oath to kill that stolid but he himself was in the terror of death. And with mixed emotions in his heart he started from his home as early as possible so that he can avoid this tragedy. And he was in such a confused state that when his mother asked that where he was going, he told her that Sakshi had called her to meet at the old fort and he is going there although it was not intended from his side to take her sister's name.

"What happened? You are feeling happy and few minutes before you were in such a state that you have lost something." Sakshi was surprised to see the sudden change in her expression.

"Your brother had called me to have a lunch together." And she passed a fake smile to her.

"Always joking! He is your friend, not your boyfriend." Sakshi passed a satire in order to tease her friend."

"I will make him my boyfriend someday."

And both girls burst into laughter.

As soon as both girls departed, Jasmine called Niharika who was already there to stay alert as Rajesh could reach there anytime. She herself hired an auto so that she could reach there before Rajesh and her friend could not find it difficult to execute her plan.

***

"Sakshi! You are here, then where is Rajesh?" Mrs. Khatri asked in a despair.

"How can I know mom. I went for a movie with Jasmine and I am coming now." She was feeling a sense of uneasiness at her mother's interrogation.

"But he told me that you called him to meet near old fort." Tension was increasing on Mrs. Khatri face.

"Mommm! Am I an insane or what that I will call him? Ok! Now let me go to my room as I have to complete some assignments." Sakshi replied in a non-caring attitude as she was frowned at her mother's questions.

"OMG! His life is in danger. Mr. Khatri! Come soon as Rajesh is in danger. Come soon." She was at the top of her voice as she had sensed that her son had been trapped.

And both sat in their car and headed for the old fort.

***

This side Niharika and Jasmine were waiting patiently for their prey as Jasmine had reached on time as expected. But Rajesh was almost tense as he was not making him understand that how can this happen that her sister would be so mean? But how will he make them apart? What would be Sakshi's feeling when she would see him? Won't she blame him for his spy nature? And with these things in mind he reached near the old fort. Not seeing any person all around he became tense. He was not getting any clue where could Sakshi be with that bastard? He started searching each and every area of the premises but then he was literally shocked to see Jasmine there and he felt a sense of comfort and uneasiness at the same time.

"What is this Jasmine?" He asked her in a frowned mood.

"I was just joking. Do you want to meet Aanand?" She was having a cachinnus on her face.

"Yes of course!" He said in a satirical tone.

And he was literally shocked to find Niharika coming from the other end. It seemed that he had frozen at the place where he was standing. The terror of fear was crystal clear in his eyes. And both girls without giving any éclair cissement shot him and made him silent permanently.

"Factum est!! " Both girls shouted in unison and hugged each other.

For the first time the girls were departing from the crime scene in a relaxed mood as they have no more tasks. But hardly had they an idea that their plan had gone through a loophole and someone was behind them. Even this side Mr. and Mrs. Khatri while getting on the stairs were stunned to see Niharika and Jasmine together.

"Jasmine! What are you doing with this witch? And where is my son?" Mrs. Khatri asked in a commanding tone.

"Uncle! Say her to behave properly. She is my friend Ruchi. And what happened to the aunty?" She said with equally commanding tone.

"Nothing has happened to her. She is right. Now I understood everything. Do you think, I will come in your fadaise. Rajesh had told me about this witch and had shown her photo to me. But hardly had he an idea that her sister's friend would be also behind this and will use her sister to set a trap for him. Tell me where my son is or I will not leave you." Mr. Khatri voice was loud and full of anger.

And when both girls sensed that the secret had been revealed, they made a quick decision by glancing into each other's eyes, they pulled down their pistols and directed towards the Khatri couples.

"We have killed that sinner whom you call your son and now we will kill both of you." They were at the top of her voice full of rage and anger.

And before the Khatri couples could react further, both girls shot them in their head and sent them to their son's destination as they were desperate for meeting to their so called son. And once again they hugged each other on the stairs.

Chapter-37

❧ ❧ ❧

Aditya Khanna was confused and tense as for the first time in his life when even after even 15 days of rigorous investigation, he was not finding any concrete. The relation between the two victims as couples had already made him confused. This side a wrapper of burqa had increased his tension. The hotel guest list doesn't show any Muslim visitor in that particular on that day in the room no. 73. Then what was the burqa doing there? There were two girls in the visitor list named Pooja and Kavita and it was not giving him any clue that why they would use burqa. And the cctv footage of hotel were displaying them as a normal girl and nothing was susceptible in nature. Even he can understand that they would have purchased it at further point of time but why they would have purchased? And even the check-out signature was same as the check-in signature and the girl were same in both cases. But one thing odd that was making his mind unsure that a girl in burqa came out of the hotel and never returned but her gait was as similar as Kavita. Then the girl in burqa was someone else or

Kavita herself? And if they were the girls only then how did they manage such a sophisticated weapon? And one thing which was confusing him that a girl came out of hotel in burqa and a girl enter the college in burqa under the name Shajia Akhtar but there was no exit signature by the same name. Then was it Kavita who was Shajia Akhtar? And if she was Kavita then how did she managed to bring Abhishek behind the bushes in the park? But there was a quite peculiar thing that one of the friend of victim was not being suspected of murder but it seemed that she was hiding something. But what it could be? And the other thing which was quite confusing that a classmate of Abhishek had seen him going in the park with a girl named Jasmine Backefield who was also her classmate in under graduation? Khanna's mind was boiling like hot water to find every time a new name added in the case. As the reports said that Jasmine had left the college after her studies and had been never seen in the campus. Then was that boy right or was there any girl who resembled to Jasmine? And when he tried to contact Jasmine, his parents said that she is in Coimbatore and is working there. But there were no any such name in the company which would suggest that she used to work there. The evidences weren't in favour of Jasmine but one thing which was sure that he didn't find any reason why she would murder Abhishek? She was neither in contact with him from the last few months and nor the ex-students were hinting any type of enmity with Abhishek.

Mr. Khanna was immersed in his thoughts in his cabin then suddenly a news broke his thought-process and the cursed news was the murder of one more Symbiosis student with his parents in Indore.

Chapter-38

❧ ❧ ❧

"Jasmine! Are you also involved in Niharika in these murders?" Mr. Backefield asked her daughter with a worried face.

"Whatt?? Is she murdering someone? How can I be with her in the murders?" Jasmine started to stumble facing this unexpected question from her father. She tried to pretend that she is unaware of the whole situation.

"Hadn't you read the morning newspaper that one more Symbiosis student is murdered along with his parents? And the name of both the students are same as you had told me the name of that morons and I am quite sure that she is killing them one by one."

She was making her face in disagreement as she can't believe her ears that Niharika could murder someone. And seeing her daughter in utter silence once again Mr. Backefield continued.

"I am damn sure that she is murdering these morons. I am in support of these murders as these droles deserved this fate. But, one thing I want to tell you Jasmine that please don't support her in murders as you will ruin your life. I can't see that my child's life would get ruined. I know that you care for your friend and you had helped her a lot. But please don't be in this mess."

Jasmine was feeling uneasy at the speech of his father and wanted it to end as soon as possible.

She was wondering that her parent's concern were right at own place but how could she make her father understand that she was not fulfilling the responsibility of a true friend but as a girl she had decided to fight against those inhumane acts which her friend had to go through. It was right that she had supported her in murdering those odurators and it could ruin her career and life but what's the use of such a life where you sit silently and become a mock spectator of those nasty activities which are happening all around your life. Of course, she was not any social reformer who had taken an oath to change the society but she can at least help those persons who are her real well-wishers. It was almost sure that her parents would consider her insane, stupid when they would get to know that her dear daughter had supported her friend in teaching those odurators a lesson but she has no repent on her decision. And she is equally determined and motivated to teach these felonious creatures the same lesson if something similar happens again.

Chapter-39

❀ ❀ ❀

This time Indore came to a standstill after getting news of the murder of three members of the same family when people got their morning newspaper. People were shocked to find that once again a Symbiosis student had been murdered along with his parents. Each and every newspaper had highlighted this murder with catchy headlines.

"Family Murdered In Old Fort"
"Shame On Symbiosis"
"One More Student Murdered"
"Are Students Safe???"
"Attack On Education"
"Why Again Symbiosis???"
"A Middle-Finger To Students"
"Faculty Murdered Along With His Son"

And these were the few headlines of the lot which were supported with very harsh articles which not only criticized the government but also the educational institutions which were failing regularly to provide safety to its' students and faculties. But perhaps the press had the slightest idea why these students and faculties are murdered; their articles wouldn't have even found mot juste in the appraisal of these brave coupe jarrets. But this is how our so called fourth pillar of the constitution works where the news are filled without research and are full of presumptions and misconceptions.

And the family which had been murdered was one of the respectable family of Indore as both husband and wife were faculties in a reputed college of Indore. People were unable to decide what are the reasons due to which Symbiosis students are murdered one by one? All the newspapers of the city was filled with the news of this sensational murder. Each and every newspaper was trying to analyse the case in its own way. Even the best of the crime analysts were unable to find any correlation between these murders. All the newspapers were trying to give the maximum coverage to this sensational murder. They were not only criticizing the law and order of society but were also vehemently attacking on the failure of the police department. As the management of the Symbiosis University had already demanded a CBI investigation into this case, the press was criticizing the government for not taking responsible and presto action into this high-profile murder case. The govt. was also facing tough criticism from opposition not to have a proper law and order in the state. There was panic all around the state as even after seven days had passed of the murder, they were neither able to find any concrete reason for the murder nor the identification of the killers had been done. The opposition was demanding the formation of a special committee and the press was demanding the identity of the killers. And the govt. was finding helpless as the murder had not been done only in his state but also in the other states and they could be accused of partiality if in case the murderer belongs from their state. And in this dilemma none of the state was forming any special committee and the press was whiplashing them regularly. All these new factors being added everyday in this case was making it almost impossible for the police department to trace the real culprit. Any would have to take the initiative and keeping these thoughts in mind the M.P Police department asked help from the central government and a special committee consisting police officers of both state was formed readily under the leadership of K.V Rangrajan. Even K.V Rangrajan was selected as the head of the committee as he didn't belonged from either of the state as he belonged to Kerala so that the government could not be further blamed by the opposition and press to have a partial attitude towards the culprits.

Chapter-40

❖ ❖ ❖

14thFebruary; Monday

And as they returned to their base camp, for the first time they had no any plans to discuss. They had not any such impasse on which they can do the brainstorming session for hours as they had no any further besoin to fulfil. And this was crystal clear on the face of both girls as even they had returned to the base camp after a period of seven days from they had completed their task. They were unable to hide this feeling for more time remaining silent and Niharika broke the ice.

"Jasmine! Now what??" She asked in a casual tone.

"Means??" Jasmine was almost in a confused state after hearing such type of question from her friend.

"Means, now when we have completed our mission, what should we do now? You will go to your home and then what will I do? Once again I will be alone." Sadness was quite crystal clear on the face of Niharika.

"Why are you taking tension? I am not going to leave you forever and you know better. We are going to enjoy a lot on the eve of completion of such a grand mission. I think you don't want to give me a grand party and that's why you are delivering such senti-talks." Jasmine tried to handle the situation as she could judge the mixed emotions reflecting in her friend's mind.

"Its' not like that! Tell me what do you want?" She said enthusiastically.

"A girl's bachelor party in which there will be only two girls." Jasmine was happy to see the changing pattern of her friend's emotions.

And then in a matter of hour there was everything on the table ranging from non-veg, different qualities of wine and few packets of cigarettes.

"That's my Nihu darling! Now we are going to enjoy for whole day and whole night." And both of them hugged each other.

As the party began they started not only to enjoy various dishes but also they were teasing each other as they used to tease each other in the college. They were wondering that how it would be when they will be caught as they will be accused of being a coupe jarret in the near future and will be allowed the same cell. But when Jasmine shared her unwillingness to talk on such topics as it would spoil their mood and the party they started to talk on unnecessary things like fashion, their favourite film stars, their friends of college and all sorts of these things which can be expected from two girls sitting alone in a room.

"Nihu! Do you drink?"

"No! Then why did you bring these bottles." She asked in a satirical tone.

"I thought you would drink." Niharika reacted as she know that Jasmine is a regular drinker.

"Ok! Leave it. Today both of us will drink as it is an important day for us and we will enjoy this day as much as possible. "Jasmine said in an assuring tone.

And even after multiple request from Niharika, Jasmine made her to drink the wine which she had brought.

"Oh no! It's very bitter." Niharika was feeling a sense of uneasiness as someone had given her any bitter medicine.

"Nothing will happen. You believe on me na baby! Look, I am also drinking." And Jasmine poured the wine in her glass and gulped it in one sip.

As the number of glasses gulped by them increased, the sensation of wine started to show its effect and rubbish talks were not uncommon.

"You know Jasmineeee, if you would have been a boy, I would have married you." Niharika voice started to stumble under the effect of wine.

"That means, I would, would have been the husband of the best girl of college, best girl of college." Jasmine was in a more stumbled situation than Niharika.

"Yeppp! Niharika weds Jasmine."

"Wow! Niharika weds Jasmine. First girl to propose any other girl directly for marriage on Valentine Day."

Both were so much under the effect of wine that they hadn't the slightest idea about what they were talking. And both girl kissed on each other's cheeks.

"Bad girlll! You don't know even how to give a kiss to your husband." Jasmine reacted as she is very unhappy from her wife and both hugged each other again.

What a night it was for Niharika! She had enjoyed the whole night without a slight degree of worry and tension on her forehead. Both slept on each other's body unaware of the whole world and what's happening behind their back.

When they got sober, the next morning once again Niharika was feeling a sense of worry that what would she do next. After their brainstorming session together for almost an hour they decided to surrender themselves in front of CBI as they considered themselves not a criminal who needs to run from police. They were wondering that why they should do such nasty activities and make their conscience low that they get the impression of a criminal themselves. And both felt a peace of mind as they were satisfied with their decision of their own course of fate which they had left in the hands of CBI to be decided. They were satisfied to be blamed by the society as a criminals but they couldn't bear the fact that anyone could accuse her of anything other else. She couldn't bear the fact that any point of time her crimes would overshadow her love once she got caught and that's why she decided to surrender herself as once she had surrendered herself in the love of that bastard.

Oh! How much pure the teenage love is?

Oh! What an irony it was! The government had handed over the case to CBI when there was no use of it. The so called culprits were going to surrender themselves and once again the CBI was going to take the credit.

Chapter-41

❋   ❋   ❋

"Sir, good morning. Am I talking to Mr. K.V. Rangrajan?" Niharika tried to assure that is she talking to the right person?

"Good morning Mam! Yes, of course. You are talking to the right person. There is nothing to N'importe. May I know whom I am talking to?" Mr. Rangrajan was surprised to get the first call of the day by a lady whose voice was extremely sweet.

"Sir, I am Niharika Ahuja and I have some very vital information regarding the murders of Abhishek and Santosh Khatri. But I can't talk on the phone as it's very much confidential and I hope you understand."

Mr. Rangrajan was almost in a shocked state as he couldn't have imagined that he will get the information so soon and so easily. Should he be happy or he should be very happy after listening this piece of news? After controlling his nerves, he tried to assure that nothing could happen with the evidence and the person giving the evidence.

"Mam, I assure that nothing will happen to you. You will be safe as earlier. Can you tell me where you are present at this time, so that we can meet and discuss upon this information. The whole information will be confidential and of course your name will." He tried to reassure the lady.

"Sir, I am currently in Gaya. You need not waste your time on Google to find me. Its' a small town located in Bihar and is famous for Bodhgaya; an international heritage site. You can reach here either by train or by flight as it boasts of having the so called international airport. I am texting you the exact address." Niharika was speaking in a row as she didn't want to waste the time as it was the part of her mission.

"Ok Mam! I will reach there in just two hours. Stay where you are and remain calm." Even Mr. Rangrajan was not understanding why this girl is so much impatient. Or is it that her life had been in danger? He couldn't ignore this fact that as she had the evidence of not only one but two very high-profile murder case and people would have been putting their best of efforts to destroy the evidence and the person. And for the first time in his career, he had demanded for a private jet from his trusted officials so that he could fulfil his commitment and save the evidence and the lady informer.

And when he reached to the airport, his mind was engrossed with different thoughts at one time. He was still not sure even in his way what could it be the case, that the day when it was announced that the case had been handled to him, he gets the informer. Or was it the case that the informer had no belief in the local police and he was waiting for the case to be handled to CBI as it is a well-known fact that CBI is far more reliable for disclosing any information rather than any government agency of our country. Or was it a trap that the killer had set for him by making the call from a lady? He was not able to judge the situation but he had to take the risk as it had already been so much late in unearthing any evidence in this case. The fact that he had been appointed is due to the fact that he is very veteran for solving peculiar cases but could he consider him enough fortunate that he has got the informer the very first day. Or someone is trying to deflect the course of investigation by calling him to such a far-flung place. But who would have been doing these things and why would he do so? If he would try to deflect him, he could have called him anywhere, then why this place? He was still doubtful and nothing was clear but he didn't want to lose this opportunity at a' tout prix.

"Sir, you reached to the address which you have told me." Then only he regained his senses. Confronting the present, he thanked the auto-driver and gave him the fare and headed towards the building.

What an impressive building it was! He felt a pleasant surprise to see such an impressive building in this small town as he had not seen any building which could impress him from the moment he stepped in the city. A single storey building built in an elegant way gave a soothing effect to the eyes. And when he rang the doorbell, he was surprised to find the gate opened in the first ring only by a beautiful lady of a tender age. Finally when he wished her good morning he was greeted with same warm but perhaps the lady was different even though the voice was much full of melody what he had listened on the phone and he was almost confident that this was not the girl whom he talked on the phone just two hours before.

"Excuse me, Mam! Is this the address of Miss Niharika Ahuja? I am Mr. K.V. Rangrajan" He wanted to make assure that he had reached to the right address even though the auto driver told him that it is the correct place.

"Oh! You are Mr. K.V. Rangrajan. Nice meeting you. Niharika is waiting inside for you." She welcomed her in that impressive building. And one thought of the officer said that she could be her sister even though he was not sure as their age almost resembled. But one thing was making him doubtful as he was not understanding why these two girls are alone in this building but he reassured his mind that her parents would have gone somewhere. It would be the reason that she would have been impatient as it wouldn't have been possible in her father's presence.

Niharika stood up from her seat and both greeted each other with a firm handshake. And when they were over with basic etiquettes of having tea and snacks, the officer came to the case.

"So, Miss Niharika Ahuja, you had told me that you have some very vital piece of information which you want to share with me in private. You can disclose the information in front of me and I can guarantee you about the confidentiality of your name." Mr. Rangrajan tried to give the talk a direction of personal care without leaving his hard-core professionalism.

"Sir, till now you would have known that we are not sisters as you would have been wondering. Till now you have known that my name is Niharika Ahuja and her name is Jasmine Backefield and we are best friends. You would have been also wondering that when I had such vital information that I want to talk you in private, then what she is doing here? Sir, before you form any misconceptions or prejudgement regarding us I should tell you that I believe on her more than myself and she is here on my meo veto..." There was a sense of professionalism even in Niharika's voice.

"I can understand." Mr. Rangrajan passed a fake smile to the girl but he was astonished that how could the girl judge her thought-process so accurately.

"Sir, before I would tell you something, I would expect that being a senior officer of the best crime agency of our country; you would listen each and everything with an open mind." Jasmine started to unearth the layer and the officer nodded his head in agreement.

"Sir, you do not need a rocket science to solve this so called mysterious case, or high-profile murder as the press had advertised. The killers are in front of you." Niharika unearthed the secret.

Mr. Rangrajan was not believing his ears on what he had heard. He couldn't haven't even dreamt in his dreams that the murders will call him themselves and admit their crime in such a relaxed state as the sense of relaxation was quite crystal clear in the eyes of both the girls. He was not literally shocked but he was almost speechless at the same moment.

And seeing the officer shocked and speechless, Jasmine continued;

"Yes! Of course, we both girls have committed these murders but before I could unearth any other thing would you tell me sir, why a person surrenders himself?"

The officer had now till now recovered from the first shock that he was getting an omen that few disguised murders had also been done and he was feeling that someone has set him on the epicentre of an earthquake zone where he is getting the harsh shocks in tits and bits. But anyhow regaining his senses, he tried to answer the question of the girls in the best possible manner.

"When a criminal feels that he has no way to escape or he is fearful of being caught and tortured; he surrender himself." He was still feeling uneasy as both the girls were gazing towards him only.

"Obviously a big **NO** to your reasons. The reasons which you gave are not sufficient to compel or better say persuade a person to surrender himself. Or it could be your so called tricks to give a wrong answer intentionally to get some more information from us as we had already said that we will unearth some other things after your reply. You had not to put any effort as we will disclose everything."

The officer was not able to understand how this Niharika could read her mind accurately everytime.

"We not only murdered these five rascals but also three another rapscallions in the different parts of the country before we had contacted you. We had intended to murder only these five mother-fuckers but the per contra situation led us to murder Neha Sinha and Mr. and Mrs. Khatri as they tried to save them." Jasmine completed her sentence in a row with pride and confidence.

The officer was almost literally shocked to hear that they have murdered three more persons and how much unfateful is that they were enquiring only on five murders.

"You would have been thinking what's the difference between the other serial killers and us who are boasting our nasty acts with pride and confidence and having no repentance on our faces? But sir, I am telling you that we are not criminals. Before, you would think that you haven't heard it for the first time, I would like to say you that we had completed our mission and we had not done anything wrong. It was our nature and conscience that prompted us not to run like criminals and surrender ourselves so that even the world can know that what compelled a girl to be a serial-killer who was enjoying her college life like every normal girl." For the first time Niharika's eyes start to moist and the officer felt pity on her. Once again Niharika continued;

"I was like any other normal girl who was enjoying the every moment of her life. I was also in love with a boy as every girl dreams of a boy who would love her unconditionally. And I was unfortunate enough to get the love of such a boy who never loved me ever and I was living in a misconception that he loves me very much. But perhaps his this ordeal was not enough for me that I got gang raped. If it would have been the victim of a gang rape I would have made my heart understand that it is the fate of some of the unfateful Indian girls as we had taken birth in the community of girls. But perhaps I was more unfateful as I became the victim of a mutual gang rape in which my own so called love invited his own friends to have a gang rape with me. As he was giving them a fabulous party to his friends, I served as a sex slave for them for the whole night. I was not only raped a multiple times but I was tortured in a way you can't even dream in your dreams. They tortured me till I got permanently unconscious and they threw me in front of a govt. hospital. The ordeal didn't end here and I went into coma and I regained my senses my after two years when I got well in a mental asylum in Ranchi. Then I found that I had not only got unconscious but also have gone mad at that time. And due to these crooks my parents suffered so much that they were just living to see me in a well-condition for the last time. They committed suicide the next morning and I was once again in depression and got well after a rigorous treatment of six months. The saddest part was that each and every real culprit was not only scot-free but was also enjoying their lives in their own way. And you're so called law and order was so much efficient that it hadn't bothered to even a look at the girl whose life had been totally devastated. Then tell me sir, what should I do? You tell me sir, what would you have done?"

Niharika was not only weeping but also there were tears in the eyes of the officer.

"Sir, at the prima facia you would have been thinking why I, Jasmine Backefield gave her full support in her mission. What would a girl do who had seen her best friend in a cheerful mode a day before and in the most inhumane condition; the next day? Being the friend of the girl who had lost each and everything in just a matter of twenty-four hours and in a situation of almost in extremis; what would have been my mindset? I have seen my friend getting rejected from her remaining family members as her parents already had committed suicide and who has gone insane almost two times? Should I have rejected her like all did or should I have supported her at that juncture of time when she was totally alone in this world? You would have been thinking why I murdered Neha Sinha and the Khatri couples. These were those crooks who even knowing the sin of their so called well-wisher tried to save them. You tell me sir, had I done anything wrong? Tell me sir." Jasmine eyes were also moist and the officer was feeling what should he tell them or what shouldn't he tell them?

"Sir, we are not asking for any apologia as crime is crime. We had narrated our reasons and now you have the arbitrium of labelling us as a serial killer or anything else?"

There was once again a sense of satisfaction in the eyes of both girls and the officer was still unsure with which name he should label these girls?

Chapter-42

❋ ❋ ❋

For the first time whole nation came to know about that so called small city when Mr. K.V. Rangrajan organised a press conference right there the next day. The whole nation was stunned to find the Deadly Duo as girls who were not only unparalleled beauty but also more deadly than they were beautiful. For the first time the officer had gone out of his protocol and allowed them to present them in public in front of the press which is considered a matter of infra dignitatem for a CBI officer. And the whole media had become like an active volcano which was trying to cover the maximum place in its paper, audio and visuals. The situation became like a typical movie where the culprits are allowed to speak in front of the press but this was the hardcore real situation where eight different persons were murdered in the different places of the country at different times by the Deadly Duo. Even the news imparted by the officer that the Deadly Duo will be present here had made the press excited and overwhelming. They were so much becoming impatient that they didn't want to listen to one of the top officer of CBI but they had no choice. They had to listen to him as he was the guy who was going to take the credit of solving this high-profile murder series as each and every victim was of the so called high-class of the society. The weather of the city had already rose to a number of degrees after hearing that the serial killers are the victims of an affaire d'amour. And the crowd was so much heavy that one wouldn't have predicted such a high degree of crowd if any film star or a sports star would have visited as in the history of this city not any press conference had been organised by any officer of CBI. People were so much fancied by this news that they were coming in swarms and even Mr. Rangrajan didn't disillusioned them as after few minutes he broke the ice and started to disclose the secrets layer by layer.

Even the introduction which those girls got by the officer made them surprised as they hadn't imagined such a humanly feeling from such a high-class professional where unprofessionalism can put your life in danger.

"Before I welcome those girls whom some of you consider as the so called **'Deadly Duo'**, witch, serial killers, murders, crooks, sinner, nasty and God knows what more. But I can't assure you 100% but I can assure 300% that you will feel that these girls are not those whom you have been embracing with your abuses and nasty words but the girls who are the angels of God. They are those girls who are obviously not common, not in the sense what you would have been wondering but different in the sense that they are an epitome of sacrifice, courage, confidence, a winning attitude, focus, truthfulness, honesty, responsibility and a lot more for which I have not the right adjectives. In my career of almost twenty-five years I met thousands of killers but neither of them got even to touch a part of my heart as I consider criminals as criminals and I don't have pity for them but these girls stole my heart. One of the girl who got gang raped and brutally tortured and had been in mental asylum for more than two years didn't lose her heart and confidence. She lost her parents in this time but she didn't make herself weep and feel miserable and decided to teach the crooks a lesson. The other girl an epitome of friendship helped her friend in the time of distress not only through her money but by all possible means and became equal partner in her friend's mission. And the unlucky girl who faced the ordeal of gang rape is only from your city and her name is Niharika Ahuja. And the girl who set an example of true friendship is from Indore and her name is Jasmine Backefield."

There was a thunderous applause and each and every person in the crowd was shouting Niharika and Jasmine in the top of his voice as he welcomed both girls to the dais.

"You would have been feeling blessed to see these two incarnations of God. You would have been wondering that may god give such daughters to every parents? Am I saying right? Yes or No?"

And there came a overwhelming response in affirmative from the crowd.

"And that's the reason crime is increasing at such a rampant society in our society. Everyone is impressed with the glorification of the crime either by the press or few persons who label themselves as a person engrossed in the deepest culture of India where forgiveness is given prime importance. Can you tell me is the murder of any person deserves forgiveness in the court of Almighty? Tell me, Yes or No?"

And there was a deadly silence where there was overwhelming cheerful crowd. Even Niharika and Jasmine were shocked by the U-turn of the officer.

"Your silence is telling me clearly that how much we are in the grasp of the glorification of crime. This is not a movie, where the culprits try to justify their murder saying that they were helpless and they are not criminals as they are on a mission. We have been used to see the murder getting a respectful bail and we come out of the theatre having a pleasant smile on our face. But this is neither a movie nor she is an actress; these both girls are hardcore professional serial killer and they had not only murdered eight people including a girl, but also the parents of one victim. They would have been thinking that they will get sympathy from me while they are trying to justify their heinous acts. How much dare they have that they called a CBI officer in their home and says with pride that they have murdered all those persons as fate had betrayed them. I can understand that they are gang raped but can anyone from the crowd tell me how many of these girls become serial killer? If you are taking the law and order in your own hands then what was the difference between those guys and these two girls? Someone in the crowd will put will their intelligent comments on law and order, but before they say something that these girls consider themselves so much smart that they didn't find necessary to even lodge an FIR in the police station. They neither lodged any complaint at the first time nor two years after when she considered herself eligible for being a serial killer. They framed new traps for each and every victim and devised the so called mind-boggling plans but they didn't have enough courtesy to lodge a complaint. They started this so called mission as their parents had committed suicide for what they had endured in the society. Each of one us knows that people have a tendency to pass comments and satires if something wrong happens in anyone's house. People also pass comments and satires on me regarding my work, then should I commit suicide and my child should become a serial killer. They give me a wired explanation why they murdered Neha Sinha whom they called in the hotel room to brainwash so that she can help her in murdering Abhishek. And when she rejected to be a partner in her crime, they shot him dead. They killed Rajesh Khatri parents' as the poor couple had seen them murdering their only son. I couldn't understand what legal punishment they should be imparted as there is perhaps no any punishment in our constitution which would match with the degree of crime they had committed? I am feeling myself in a morally down situation filled with shame in my heart as how could it be ungrateful that I had confronted such a criminal who is not even eligible to call themselves an animal? As everyone one of us knows that even the animals or the demons do not commit such a low degree of activity which could make the humanity shameful."

And alas! What is the nature of the common masses we all know? The crowd which was cheering and overwhelming in favour of these girls half an hour before were cursing these girls for being such a demon.

But even at the time when the tables had turned they were not having any repentance on their face as they were convinced of what they had done. They were already ready for such a U-turn of the officer as we all know for this thing only our law and order is notorious for? They were not so much feeble that they would have broken at such a speech given by person who is of such a low mentality. They had listened their heart at that time also and even this time and they were completely satisfied. And they headed to the CBI headquarters for further interrogation.

Chapter-43

❋ ❋ ❋

Mr. K.V Rangrajan got a warm welcome after he reached the CBI headquarters. Even the best of the officers were stunned to hear the speech by the officer. They were exclaimed at how the officer handled the situation. At one time when they heard the first part of his speech they were exclaimed what had happened to the officer? They were wondering that had he caught in the charm of young girls or had they offered him something special which couldn't be ignored as the criminals are ready to offer anything for being saved and anything means anything. But when they heard his second part then they understood that why Mr. K.V. Rangrajan had got the name K.V. Rangrajan. He was really the **'Rajan of Rang'** (Master in changing colours) and he had really shed his colours so ghastly that no one was able to understand. At one time he was showing such type of sentiments with them that he was not only feeling pity for them but also there resides a heart inside this hardcore CBI officer who is so much kind-hearted and a respect for the criminals if they made him assure that they were helpless. But this was K.V. Rangrajan who was such a shrewd officer that the best of the mind readers couldn't predict his mind. And his this quality had made him rose in the department. He had only one thing in mind while confronting a criminal that you have to be in total synchronization with the criminal and then it's your time to play your part. And he had done the same thing with these girls. When these girls were narrating their story by putting their confidence in him he was thinking something else and whenever these girls tried to predict his thought-process he pretended such as he had been caught. And now the officer was wondering how these girls can get the death penalty as for him the only punishment for a murder was death penalty and nothing else.

***

How much shrewd would be the CBI officer would be, but there were a lot of people who felt a connection with these girls. Obviously there were a lot of people who were swayed by the later part of the speech of the officer but also there were persons who felt pity for these girls. But as the common man is a common man and he can do nothing more than discussing any sensational or sensitive topics in his drawing room or on his tea table and they became a topic of hot discussion in the whole nation. And as it have been a tendency that some of the agency or organisations of our country grab a topic for fulfilling their legitimate or illegitimate interest and there started protests all over India in against and favour of these girls. There were agencies that really had either a good or bad feeling towards these girls and they had decided either to protest in against or favour of these girls. But a lot of agencies, organisations and political parties made their entry into this game just to remain in limelight. Whatever would be the case, for the first time in the history of the nation a serial killer or better say **'Deadly Duo'** was getting response in favour from the whole country.

People are least surprised when they find same political party in against and favour in any similar case but the most surprising case were the so called women welfare organisations. The women welfare organisations which mostly consist of women at the top positions and boast of women empowerment were against the "Deadly Duo". Those organisations who make a lot of hue and cry whenever a girl is raped about the degrading position of women's in the society were today labelling these girls as shame for humanity. They were considering those girls as a shame for humanity who were not gang raped but a victim of mutual gang rape. And anyone could understand that a girl would be more torn apart if she is the victim of the mutual gang rape. Someone had rightly said that women are the biggest enemies of women. If it not have been the case these so called women caring agency would not have considered them brutal murderers even after knowing the cause why they committed the crime. The organisations which consider themselves as a means of getting away from the dungeon of male tyranny were today indirectly supporting them as they were accused of trying to have a pre-marital sex. These angels of god who make protest whenever a person having diseased mentality announces in the public that girls should not wear short clothes as they inflame sensuality in boys; had they ever thought before going against these girls that their dual mentality is causing the girls to face such an outrageous catastrophe like mutual gang rape. This was the courage and efforts of these girls that she had tried to fight with their whole effort against this catastrophe otherwise God knows how many girls in our country are torn apart every year and the traitors whom they were advocating treat the girl as a material of their birthday party. These girls have only one fault and that fault is that they love one of these sybaritics and he feels the privilege to give the reward of her love by using the girl as a sex salve or a material of enjoyment on his birthday party.

Chapter-44

❖ ❖ ❖

As there were protests all over the country, so it was the direst responsibility of Mr. K.V. Rangrajan that the court hearings and the judge decision shouldn't be affected by these swarms of people. It's a common phenomenon in our country to organise a fast track court for high-profile murder or a rape case and unfortunately it came under both category and a fast track court was organised just in a matter of seven days after clearing the initial proceedings. How much a person is shattered when he finds that whom he consider his life is away from you when he is needed the most? And Jasmine broke into tears finding that her parents are not coming into hearing. Niharika consoled her and headed towards the courtroom where the media of the whole country and lots of people either in against or favour was present there. The whole nation's eyes were fixed on this high-profile case.

And without any delay, the court proceedings started formally.

But even before the swearing ceremony could start, people were stunned to find that Niharika rose from her seat and people were terrified as they were unsure about any mishappenings which can happen there instantly.

"My Lord! As everyone here present in this courtroom knows what we had done and I wonder that why you should waste your time on these waste arguments between the so called the most intelligent people of our constitution. My lord; we do not want to waste our time on those craps which neither you want to listen nor we want to answer and we are requesting you to pass your judgement and save this time for those girls who are torn apart more than us and are unlucky enough to get cito sound judgement. My Lord! Please utilise this time for giving the judgement to the unlucky girls who are being intentionally trapped by these dark coat claded professionals who try to humiliate us more than that mother-fuckers by their dark questions on the name of fair trial and so called getting details for reaching to the reality. Before they ask me such questions like an absurd guy that how, what and why they did to me or had I enjoyed at that moment which would let me fill with anger and rage please pass your judgement. Please pass your judgement before these shameless professionals would try to torn our heart with their audacious questions which they will ask without having a stain of regret on their face. It might happen that they will prove that licentious rascals innocent and label us as Dames de la halle and would ask for the highest possible penalty for our crimes but My Lord! Please don't allow these brazen professionals to celebrate the opportunity of asking such idiotic questions which will not only compel us to kiss the dust but also would bring once again shame for those girls who had been already deteriorated by the bloody butchers already. Before they label us as cunning, deviant, lecherous, prostitutes, heinous and a lot more please pass your judgement as soon as possible. My Lord! I know I am ready to be labelled anything and everything but I know they will not feel a stain of remorse on their forehead in labelling my love as a false love, lustful love and God knows what more, so please punish us before my love for that lewd bastard would get also an object of mockery in front of the whole nation. My love was not an object of mockery even though we had been compelled to transform it into such state. My Lord! Please save my love for that bloody butcher to be loaded with satirical allegories by punishing us as soon as possible.

The whole court including the judge was stunned to hear such words from these girls and they were almost sure that it was the shortest case in the Indian constitution which got over before it could start after reaching the courtroom.

And after thinking for some time, the judge spoke;

"The culprits have already accepted his crime and requested for judgement but even though we are giving them a time of two days to rethink upon it and the court is adjourned for today as the final hearing will be after two days."

Chapter-45

✤ ✤ ✤

Once again both girls were in the news for their extra frank behaviour in the courtroom. Some were suspecting it as their trick and someone were saying it right not to waste the time of the court. There were buzz all around the nation on the reason of her such extra frank behaviour. And this side even K.V. Rangrajan was unsure as he had not expected such type of foolishness from these imperious girls. He was wondering that it may be their conscience that had prompted them to surrender but what was it that happened in the court? Or they had been trapped? It couldn't be ignored that they would have been threatened or something else. But his sixth sense was almost sure that they were the killers. But the million-dollar question was why? Why? And finding no answers, he was frustrated. It was not the case that the officer was frustrated or something but everyone associated with it was tense. The political parties were tense as they were going to lose an oven where they can prepare their political chapatti and the so called women empowerment agencies were tense because they were losing an extra important issue very soon. Jasmine parents were already in tension after the news and this information had made them tense.

But there was a sense of relaxation on two faces and there is no need to explain that these two faces were Niharika Ahuja and Jasmine Backefield. They were feeling relaxed as this whole drama will get over soon and they could meet their unexpected end expectedly.

Epilogue

❖ ❖ ❖

Present Day (11ᵗʰMarch; 10:30 A.M)

"Hey! You two witches! Now your time is over. Come with me." The prison officer came once again and hinted to get up from there and come along with him.

Confronting the present, they passed a gentle smile to the prison officer as he is doing a favour on them which made the officer awkward.

"I know you two are really wicked. You can smile together as you can for more five minutes. After that you will be issued a death penalty and you will be allotted different cells, then I will see how much you smile on me." And he gave a nasty look to these girls.

Once again they passed a smile to him.

Today the court was packed more than it was on the first day. Even though it was tightly packed up to the roofs, people present there were already sure that this proceeding is not going to last for more than fifteen minutes. The formal proceedings of the court started. Today the judge decided to pass his judgement without any previous hassles which could make the courtroom awkward.

"As you know you both are autre fois convicts and before I pass my judgement, once again I would like to ask from you that does any of you want to say anything?"

People were expecting nothing from these girls but were astonished to get an affirmative reply from Niharika. After the mandatory swearing ceremony, Niharika started;

"My Lord! Even before I should start saying anything, and the gentlemen sitting in this courtroom make any false impression about us I would like to say that we both girls whom the whole nation had labelled us by different adjectives were the same girls as we were earlier. I would like to save your time by telling you in advance that Jasmine is not going to say anything and please don't waste the time by asking her to speak anything. And the reason that she will not speak as Jasmine consider me as a part of her soul and when one part of soul is speaking there is no need to waste the time by repeating the same thing. She always tells me that we both are one and we will remain always one and I am saying these words with the ad arbitrium of my Jasmine."

People were feeling confused that what she was talking about. And the CBI officer was feeling that these words are coming out of fear.

"You would have been wondering why I am always talking about saving time? The first thing is that I do not like to waste the time of honourable court and the other reason is that people do not waste their mind in reading our eyes that how much fearful we are regarding our fate. I should assure them that we are not fearful regarding our fate.

My Lord! We are very much fearful and as everyone knows that girls are fearful in nature and if anyone is saying that we are not fearful is telling a lie. Yes we are fearful! We are fearing that when the time will come when a girl even think upon to love any guy unconditionally? How would a girl dare to be immersed in a guy's love so much that she would not consider her own image and reputation between her friends? I am fearing how a girl would find the reason to let his heart immersed into any other guy's love? Will any girl dare to risk her career so that she could deserve the utmost care of a guy for whom she is ready to do everything? I am fearing why our so called scholars and philosophers advertise the love as a virtue. My Lord! What would you say about that girl who came from a different city to make her life more beautiful as it was earlier and she finds an intimacy towards this so called virtue? I would not tell you our story as you know our story better than us but tell me one thing who is that person who said that if you love anyone you get love in return? Go and tell that person what a girl like me gets in the return of love? She became just an object of zeit vertreib for a bunch of lecherous impostors. I am fearing what this girl standing in front of me would have felt when she would have seen me in such a terrific condition? I am fearing what would have those parents felt when they would have got to know that her child had been gang raped."

Her voice was getting louder with each and every words.

"Yes, My Lord! I am fearing of the condition of that girl who would have seen her friend struggling for her life for six months even after she had spent her life in a mental asylum for almost two years. I am fearing that what would be the thought-process of a girl who wants to start a new life after such ordeal and is considered as a whore who are blot on the society by the doctors of the asylum itself? I am fearing what would the girl think when she finds that she has not been in mental asylum for treatment as her parents had expected, instead the asylum officials are using her as a sex slave till the time she get recovered. And this inhumane news is delivered by the officials themselves as they are sure that no one is going to believe that girl as she had already been a victim of mutual gang rape and the society had already labelled her as a characterless whore."

There was pin drop silence in the courtroom as no one was there who would not feel the injustice which had happened to that girl.

"Our respected CBI officer said that if I would have loved him truly, I wouldn't have murdered him. Mr. Rangrajan; you could be the best officer of this country and you could be a great investigator. I know you can go to any depth of the crime to find evidence, then please go and find how deeply I loved him. If you want to know the depth of my love; go to my city, go to my college and ask anyone who knows me and then you will know how deeply I used to love that impudent turpid. The bastard who was once the reason of my smile; snatched my smile for forever. He not only snatched my smile but my parents and my Jasmine. Obviously I would be labelled as a witch who one time says that I love him deeply and the next moment I am abusing him as I have just hatred for him but I had also loved someone who was not only the reason of my smile, but he was everything for me.

My Lord! I am not a serial killer or anything like that. I have just gave them their deserved punishment for what they had done. And I am standing here in front of you as I had also loved someone."

There was complete silence in the room and lots of eyes were moist hearing the story of this girl but before anyone could sense anything even the judge himself, both girls consume cyanide and met their respectful end.

ABOUT THE AUTHOR

A voracious reader, keen observer, feminist culminated together defines Nitish Raj. Based in Hyderabad he basically belongs from Bihar. He remained quite a bright student throughout his academic career before dropping his MBA in order to satiate his hunger for writing. Not only he is passionate about writing fiction but also loves to write opinion-editorials and non-fiction articles on social issues related to women empowerment, gender equality, caste system and social transformation. A firm believer in the serenity of the solemn virtue, he is keen about writing the dark truth of the society which have been sidelined in our quest of happy endings.

This is his first published novel